GHOST DOG
OF
KILLICUT

By the same author
Run, Rainey, Run
Ironhead
Softly Roars the Lion

GHOST DOG
OF
KILLICUT

By Mel Ellis
Illustrated by Dick Amundsen

Four Winds Press · New York

Second printing, 1970

Published by Four Winds Press
A Division of Scholastic Magazines, Inc., New York, N.Y.
Text copyright © 1969 by Mel Ellis.
Illustrations copyright © 1969 by Scholastic Magazines, Inc.
Printed in the United States of America.

Library of Congress Catalogue Card Number: 70-81696

In memory of Charles (Chuck) Morgan

Trainer and handler of three national champion retrievers and a friend of every one of the thousands of dogs which once passed through his kennels.

1

I stood at the wheel of my big boat, the *Killicut*, looking into the spray for safe passage through Death's Door — a narrow, rockbound cut of water between two islands. Lake Michigan was in a turmoil. The wind blew with tumultuous force. It howled through the high rocks jutting out of the water and sent foam from the breakers streaking around me like snow. My black Labrador, Muggsy, was on a seat across from me. She was clawing to stay on the narrow shelving so I said a few words to reassure her, but the wind whipped the sound from my mouth and hurled it south across the waves.

It was then I saw the ghost, the phantom dog everybody had been talking about. He was standing on the very tip of Red Island on a slab of white rock, staring out across the wild water. I was astounded, because he

7

did look like an apparition, except that when he moved I *knew* he was a real flesh and blood dog, a black Labrador like Muggsy, only twice as big.

Inky black as the sky above, he seemed almost unaware of the wind, except that his ears were back a little and his tail was tucked more tightly between his legs than he might normally have carried it. He was so shiny wet that when he shifted his weight from one front paw to another I could see the muscles ripple like ropes under his hide. His head was held high and beneath his chin was a surprising white spot which glistened almost as if it were phosphorescent.

Muggsy must have seen him too, because I saw her ears move forward to an alert position. She lifted her muzzle but if she howled the wind carried the sound south and I never heard it.

Sight of the dog made me forget about the reef. For weeks I had been hearing about him from other fishermen, men on ore boats and the ferry. But even their stories hadn't prepared me, because I just couldn't believe such a majestic dog really did exist. He looked like a sculptor's creation, a great dog cut from a block of black granite with every feature larger than life. No wonder they said he was a ghost. No wonder from the city of Green Bay all the way north to Washington Island, they told such stories about him.

I had to will myself to take my eyes from the dog, and then it was almost too late. I was on the threshold of Death's Door and in another minute the wind would have run me on the rocks. I swung hard on the wheel to bring the bow straight into the wind. I gave her full throttle, but there was no quick response because the wind and the waves were hard and pushing. The *Killicut* wallowed, and I thought she would turn from the wind to go crashing. Other boats had, and on a calm day a man could look through the clear water down at the broken ribs of boats that hadn't made it.

But the *Killicut* was a good boat. Her screw took hold, bit into the water. It lifted her knife-sharp bow and she sliced the waves. Then we were out of the cut and when I looked back the dog was gone.

Right then, although it was only moments ago that I had seen the dog, I began to have a strange feeling which grew until I wasn't really sure I had seen a black Labrador with a white chin. By the time I had brought the *Killicut* to safe harbor and eased her alongside the dock in front of my little green house, I was almost convinced that the wind and waves had played tricks with my mind and my eyes and I had, as everyone was saying, seen only the ghost of a dog.

I had no fish to unload this day, because alone I hadn't been able to raise the nets in the high wind. So I tied down the boat and went up to the house to clean up. Thoughts of the dog went quickly from my mind, because this was the day I had to see Gear Callahan about renewing my note, and I was afraid that he would refuse.

Callahan is branch manager of the village of Killicut Bank which has its main offices in Green Bay. When I bought the *Killicut*, I had put five hundred dollars down on her, and the bank had loaned me the rest. If I didn't meet the note when it was due, they could either give me more time or take the *Killicut*. Lately they had been getting tough and I was scared.

For one thing, my age was against me. I was only eighteen. John, my Milwaukee brother and guardian (both our folks were dead), was my boss until I was twenty-one. He had cosigned the note for me.

"I'll sign," he had said, "but I think you're nuts to want to stay up there and try to make a go of fishing, especially the way fishing has been."

My other two brothers thought I was nuts too. Pete, a pharmacist in St. Louis, and Joe, a dentist in Chicago, had both said they'd finance my education if I'd just ditch the notion of wanting to dredge a living out of the sometimes treacherous big lake.

"Look, Guy," they both said (my name is Guy Hardin), "the fishing in Lake Michigan has been going downhill for the last thirty years. Where once there were fleets of boats, today there isn't a fisherman. So how are you going to make it go? How are you going to make a living doing what Dad nearly starved to death trying to do?"

They were right about one thing. Dad had had a rough time of it toward the end of his life. But what they didn't seem to realize is that Lake Michigan was in for a re-birth, that some day (and I figured that day wasn't too far distant) she'd be producing again the way she'd never produced before.

I thought about it on my way down to the bank with Muggsy. The wind still howled and women on the street were hanging onto their dresses and men were holding onto their hats. It was a real northeaster coming right across the ten islands of the Raspberry group into Killicut Harbor and throwing water darn near up into the main street.

Callahan had someone in his office so I waited and talked to his secretary, Natalie Parish. Natalie knew about my dreams. We had been in high school together. She was a soft sort of person with warmth in her big brown eyes and in her long brown hair. But she was a no-nonsense girl and I liked her for it.

Her father had been a fisherman, but then when the fish disappeared he was lucky to get a shipyard job in Sturgeon Bay. But his heart wasn't in it, and Natalie often told me he felt like a boat in a boneyard dying from dry rot.

Natalie was my girl, if you could say I had a girl. There wasn't much between us. There couldn't be. Not with the prospects I had.

Once I got up and went to the door to look out to see if Muggsy was waiting. She went everywhere with me, and now she sat patiently, the wind tossing her ears and sometimes running the hairs along her back right up on end.

When I turned around Natalie said I could go in. Callahan was behind a big desk lighting his pipe. He motioned me to a chair and when I sat down he said: "Well, Guy, and how's the fishing?"

I didn't answer his question, but got right to the point. "I've got a hundred dollars for you," I said, "but that's all I could raise this time."

Callahan, once a fisherman himself, looked down at his calloused hands. Then he looked up at me from beneath shaggy brows and said quietly: "That's only about half the interest that's due, Guy, and you haven't paid a penny on the principal in the year you've had the *Killicut*."

I felt my throat going tight and my mouth going dry. But I sat straighter and leaned forward a little. "You know it's been a tough year," I said.

Callahan looked up at the ceiling as though he didn't want to look into my eyes. He had a weather-beaten face, and like most fishermen, he found it hard to be stern. But he got on with it anyway and said: "It's been a tough forty years, Guy. You're in a losing business. I think you ought to sell the boat. There are plenty of guys who would make a pleasure craft out of her. Then you'd come out with your five hundred and be able to get started in something else."

That's what they all told me! Get out! My brothers. Gear Callahan. Even the two fishermen in Killicut who were still running boats and hanging on by the skin of their teeth.

"If we weren't stuck with all this equipment," the other Killicut fishermen said, "do you think we'd keep on fishing?"

Everybody claimed I was being plain foolish. "You're young," they would say, "and you don't have to be a fisherman. You can be anything you want to be. This is the age of opportunity!"

But I had my dream. I'd told Callahan before, but now I told him again: "Mr. Callahan, I don't want to be anything except a fisherman. The day is coming, and it isn't far off, when fishing in Lake Michigan is going to be terrific, and when it comes I want to be ready to take advantage of it."

He put up a hand to stop me. He didn't want to hear it all again. He didn't want to hear me tell him that the lake trout, gone since the 1930's, were coming back now that the federal government had whipped the lamprey eel problem, killed off the snakelike creatures which sucked the life out of the trout. He didn't want to hear my same old pitch about how the walleyed pike and the perch were coming back, about the almost miraculous populations of rainbow trout and cohoe salmon that were showing up since they'd been planted.

But I leaned forward and told him again anyway, and I added: "They're even cleaning up the rivers so the old lake is bound to get better. Look, Mr. Callahan, I had a hundred pounds of cohoes in my nets the other day. Think of what that will mean when we can harvest them!" I was leaning so far forward I almost fell out of my chair.

"But will they open the season for commercial fishermen?" Callahan asked. "Or will they leave the trout and the salmon for sport fishermen? And if they do open the season, when will it happen? In five, maybe ten years? By that time you'll starve to death, and if I make more loans to fishermen, so will I!"

But I couldn't see it. Alewives, a shiny little ocean fish, had come down the St. Lawrence waterway into the Great Lakes. It was like manna from heaven for the trout and the salmon. The big fish grew enormous by feeding on the billions of alewives, and I dreamed of the day when there wouldn't be just the *Killicut,* but a whole fleet — maybe ten — of fishing boats. I'd call it the Killicut Crew Company and have my own refrigeration trucks and packing houses and maybe even my own stores across the country for selling Killicut Crew Company Fresh Fish.

It was a big plan for an eighteen-year-old, and it seemed I was the only one who had it. The old-timers, those still fishing, were content with enough trash fish to keep the wolf from the door, and they only dreamed about the good old days instead of looking ahead to the wonderful days that were coming.

I believed in my dream. Nights lying in bed I'd see Killicut Harbor the way she used to be with maybe fifteen or twenty outfits running boats. I tried to get Callahan to believe. I had to get Callahan to believe.

I couldn't go to my brothers. They couldn't see it any more than Callahan. "Any amount," they'd shout at me, "for an education or some other business. But not one darn dime for a dying business, for a business that all but killed Dad!"

I tried again to convince Callahan. "Look, Mr. Callahan," I said, "our congressmen in Washington, our governor, and our lawmakers right here in Wisconsin — all of them — are fighting to clean up the lake. They're going to do it! The fish are already coming back. I know it! All a man has to do is hang on."

Sometimes I wondered though. There were days when the nets were empty. If it hadn't been for the smelt run — another silvery little fish which came down the St. Lawrence waterway from the ocean — I'd not have made enough money to eat last spring. Only the chubs coming to net, the chubs and the smelt, saved me.

The house was part mine, so my brothers were letting me live in it rent free. But they'd wanted to sell, because they said property values on the peninsula were going down.

Callahan got up. He was short as I was — short and muscular with big shoulders for pulling nets and hanging onto a line while the boat backed over the anchor so it could be hoisted. "Look, Guy," he said, finally looking directly at me, "banks can't go financing dreams or they'd go out of business. I know how you feel, and that's why I'm not going to foreclose on you and take the boat away now."

For a minute I felt a surge of hope. He had said he wasn't going to take the boat. But my hope died when he continued: "I'm going to give you ninety more days. I expect you to make arrangements during that time to sell the boat yourself so maybe you can show some profit on your five-hundred-dollar investment. All we want is our two thousand dollars plus the interest. Anything over and above is yours, but if we are forced to handle the sale, chances are you'll never make out as well as if you handled it yourself."

Then he sat back down and shoved a new note across the desk for me to sign. There was nothing to do except to sign. Ninety days wasn't much, but it was better than nothing. Things sometimes happen fast. Maybe, just maybe, I'd find a way.

I thanked Callahan though I didn't feel thankful, and then I turned and started toward the door. Just as I was opening it he called out: "Wait," he said. I turned. He was holding a section of newspaper toward me. I could see that it was *The Milwaukee Journal*. "Find this dog," he said, "and your problems are solved."

I walked slowly back and took the paper from him. The heading on the story read: "$3,000 Reward Offered for Lost Dog." Then — and I could hardly believe my eyes — right alongside the story was a picture of the black Labrador I had just seen, white chin patch and all!

"That's . . . that's the . . . the . . ." I almost told him, but I shut my mouth in time.

Callahan was laughing. "I'm just kidding," he said, "that dog has to be dead. He was lost more than a month ago. People must be seeing his ghost."

I didn't know if Callahan was kidding or not — about the ghost I mean. I didn't figure he was one to believe in ghosts, but I didn't wait around to ask him. I wanted to get out of there, to go off somewhere to read the story alone. It seemed too impossible.

I only nodded to Natalie when I walked past and then I slid through the door out into the wind. Muggsy rubbed her head against my knee to tell me she had missed me, and we started up the street for the Safe Harbor Inn.

There was an empty booth in back and I sat there

alone. When Mattie Schofield came over I ordered a Coke and then I laid the newspaper in front of me and began to read the story.

"Charles (Chuck) Morgan today posted a $3,000 reward for the return of his world champion Labrador retriever, Jet's Black Flash. The dog, lost while Morgan was hunting the Lake Michigan Raspberry Island Chain, in addition to winning the national retriever trials was judged best of show at the recent International Dog Bench Show.

"Morgan, president of Sweet Grain Breweries here, has been a Labrador breeder since the dogs were first imported to this country many years ago. He is usually credited with having done more for the breed than any man in the country.

"The dog, larger than standards usually acceptable for bench, and having a white chin patch never before seen in Labradors, made such an impression on the judges that they waived the rules in naming Jet winner.

"Morgan claims the animal is the sole link in a breeding chain he has perpetuated. The breed is characterized by a white chin patch.

"The dog was lost when it followed a crippled golden-eye duck out into the storm-tossed lake. Search parties have combed the islands and, though scores of people report having seen the large black dog, none have gotten close enough to put a rope on it.

"Fishermen and the Coast Guard along Wisconsin's Door County Peninsula believe the dog is dead. They don't believe the dog could survive on the islands. But, as sometimes happens, people are not going to let the dog die. They are quoted as saying that a dog with so great a heart must live on even when its body dies.

"Morgan scoffs at the ghost stories, at the tales of a black spirit roaming the islands. He claims Jet could survive.

" 'If people are seeing a big, black dog,' Morgan said, 'they are not seeing a ghost. They are seeing Jet in the flesh.' "

I rolled up the paper and I was almost out of the door when Mattie called: "Guy, you forgot to pay." I reached in my pocket, fished out a dime, and handed it to her. Then as I was closing the door I heard her say: "What's the matter with him? He didn't touch his Coke."

And I remembered that I hadn't, because I had my mind on that dog. If he was out there on those islands I was the guy who could get him — if anybody could!

17

2

During the night the wind had worn itself out. At dawn the harbor was glass smooth and there were ice edges in the backwaters to catch the glint of the sun. I was nearly out of the harbor by the time the sun was high enough to lay a ribbon of shine on the water.

Bill Bratton was with me. He helps me sometimes so that he can make a little wine money, only I have to catch him sober to get him to work. He had run out of money yesterday so when I knocked he stood shivering in his long underwear at the door, sleepy-eyed but anxious to go.

I didn't tell Bill about the dog. I wasn't going to tell anyone. I meant to pull the last two nets I had out and concentrate on finding that Labrador. With three thousand dollars to start the season next spring I'd have the boat paid for. Then I could start saving for another, and someday perhaps another, so when the fishing was good again I'd be ready with a fleet of boats, and maybe I'd be the number-one fisherman on the peninsula.

The *Killicut*, a shining white twenty-three footer, was like a thing alive this morning. I had only to touch the throttle and I could feel the deck move under me as she leapt forward to cut a trench for herself through the water.

As we neared Death's Door I turned the wheel over to Bill and climbed to the top of her compact little cabin where the flag Natalie had made for me flew. Stitching on the flag was her idea — the North Star with a long line anchoring it to the ground. Explaining it, she had said: "You're always hanging your hopes on a star so I thought it would be appropriate." The anchor was her idea too. She said: "It means no matter how sky-high your dreams take you, it's a good idea to keep your feet on the ground."

Of course, Natalie wasn't the only one who thought I had dreams which were beyond realization. Maybe that's the way it was with me. Maybe I had to have my dream or there was nothing.

I braced myself on the cabin roof and stood erect so I could scan the shores of Green and Red islands. Except for the gulls and itinerant flocks of ducks there were no signs of life so I came down. I took the wheel from Bill and nosed the *Killicut* into Death's Door. When I felt the current grab her I gave her all the gas she'd take and we slipped through like a sliver and came popping out on the other side of the reef.

We lifted the two nets and took a couple of boxes of chubs. Then I hit for the harbor to sell the fish and get rid of Bill so I could get started that afternoon hunting for the dog.

19

When I got to shore, Luke Morrisson, a drinking partner of Bill's, was standing on the dock. "Millie says to call your Milwaukee brother collect," he said as the *Killicut* came gently to dockside. Millie was the local telephone operator.

"Thanks, Luke," I said. I asked him to help Bill take care of the fish, and I handed him fifty cents and gave Bill a dollar.

I suppose I could have ignored the telephone call. I knew why John wanted to talk to me. Callahan had undoubtedly called him to say he'd given me another ninety days. My brother would have to cosign the note, which meant he would have to make good on the boat if I didn't.

But I needed his signature, so I went into the house and put in the call. "Guy, how are you going to live this winter?" John believed in getting right to the point.

"Well, I thought I might be able to get a job working in the woods," I said into the receiver. "Messmer's Crew is going to be cutting a lot of pulp, and I guess maybe he'll give me a job."

"You guess. You guess. You guess at everything!"

To make him feel better I said: "Well, if I can't go to work for Messmer's Crew, maybe I'll come to Milwaukee and look for a job."

"Now you're talking sense," John said. He and all my brothers wanted me off the peninsula. They always remembered what the fishing had done to Dad. They couldn't believe there were opportunities right here in Killicut. When I didn't say anything more, John continued: "Callahan called. About the note. Why don't you let them have the boat? When they sell it you'll get your five hundred back — or most of it."

I knew I couldn't argue over the phone about how I

20

felt it would be the biggest mistake of my life to give up before I had hardly gotten started, so I lied, but only a little. I said: "I think I can sell her myself and maybe make a profit on my five hundred if I put in some work and fix her up."

I could hear his sigh plainly as though he was in the house with me instead of nearly two hundred miles away in Milwaukee. "Okay, Guy," he said, "but this is the last time I sign. So you'd better start looking for a customer."

"How's the family?" I asked, trying to get him off the subject of the boat.

"Fine, Guy. Fine. And you?"

"Never better!" And it wasn't exactly a lie, because the sight of the dog out on the island had given me new hope.

"You take care now," John said, and then he hung up.

Well, I had my ninety days. Three months and then I'd have to come up with more than a thousand dollars to pay the interest and principal I'd missed. Well, if I caught the dog . . .

That's the way I was dreaming and it startled me to notice suddenly that I was sitting there with the telephone receiver still in my hand. I put it down softly and went outside. Muggsy was on the stoop soaking up sun, but she jumped to her feet when she heard the door.

"Come on, Mugs," I said to her, "we're going hunting."

The sun was warm for November and I stood at the wheel without a jacket, watching the gulls glide along back of the boat hoping for fish entrails. The exhaust left a little blue trail at the water line and the engine sounded solid, as though she'd just come out of the factory and was on her maiden run.

As the long curving crescent of ten islands grew larger, I wondered what strategy I'd use to catch the big dog. It would be a job. The smallest of the ten islands of the Raspberry group is about three acres. The largest, Blue Island, is at least a hundred acres. It's heavily wooded, has two small lakes on it, and since it is designated as a game refuge hunters never invade it.

Blue Island has a large deer herd and a variety of smaller animals and birds. Sometimes the deer trade islands, but they always go back to Blue, because the others have been so whitewashed with gull droppings that all vegetation has died. Even the trees are dead. To me these lesser islands look like old battlefields where shells have exploded all the foliage to kingdom come.

I don't know the real names of the islands (if they ever had any), but the natives call them all by color. In addition to Red, Green, and Blue, there is Black, White, Yellow, Purple, Orange, Brown, and Gray. Why colors for names? Don't ask me. None of them resemble the colors they were named after. With the exception of Blue, all the islands are stark white. I suppose there were just so many stringing out there that instead of numbering or naming with the usual sort of names, somebody decided it would be prettier to call them by colors.

Blue, the big island, once had people living on it. But that was years ago when fishing was good and the boats put into a harbor on the south side to be nearer the fishing grounds. Maybe someday I'd live out there. Maybe I'd even buy the island and then maybe I'd change the name to Hardin's Island.

I slipped the *Killicut* through Death's Door and then I swung her south and came to a natural harbor on the backside of Red, the island on which I'd seen the dog. I couldn't get the boat through the shallows to shore, so

I anchored her, slipped on waders, and went over the side to walk to the beach. Muggsy jumped and swam alongside me.

Up on the slabs of white rock high above the water line, I took off the waders and slipped into the low boots I'd carried. Then I started for the tip of the island which borders one side of Death's Door.

I was looking for tracks. Ghosts don't leave tracks, and though I didn't believe the stories that were going around about how the dog was already long dead, I had to convince myself. But there were no tracks, not a one, and I walked the muddy stretches and the sandy stretches and even tried to find some sign among the cobblestones and on the flat slab rocks. But there was nothing.

Of course, I told myself, the storm could have blotted out any sign along the shore. That had been quite a blow and it had rained and even snowed a little. But it was spooky not to find even one track where yesterday I'd seen the big dog standing.

I stood on the edge of Death's Door watching the current go swirling through the cut. It's the only place a boat can get through. The underwater reefs from island to island are all too close to the top, and in dry years a man might wade them traveling from Blue to Gray to White or whichever, except he can't ever cross the cut people call Death's Door.

Some captains won't shoot through the cut. Maybe they remember the boats which hadn't made it and the bodies which had washed ashore. But to go all the way around the string of islands is a long haul and a fisherman could lose hours of time.

The cut had never bothered me and I turned my back on it and walked to the center high point of the island.

I had a whistle with me, a shrill whistle like the ones used at field trials. It had occurred to me that Jet, having been trained on a whistle, just might come to the sound of one.

When I was high enough so I could see in both directions along the beach, I blew. The gulls lifted shrieking. A flock of black ducks feeding in a cove arose, quacking. Muggsy came running up to me and sat with a quizzical look on her face. I felt foolish then, standing there with the shiny whistle in my hand, because I could just hear what some townsfolk would be saying if they knew: "And there the darn fool stood in the middle of that long string of islands trying to whistle up a ghost."

I put the whistle back into my pocket and was starting back toward the boat when something caught my eye. It was down the beach a ways moving in the slight wind. I knew it wasn't the dog, but I also knew that it was something that didn't belong there.

I started down the beach keeping my eyes open for signs of a dog's passing. The closer I got to the strange object, the more it looked like nothing other than a rag caught on a bush, a dirty, gray rag waving in the wind.

When I got to it I saw it was a gull long dead. Somehow or other, it had gotten its neck caught in the fork of a branch and strangled itself. Now it was nothing but feathers and bones, and I took it as a sharp reminder that fooling around on the islands in November wasn't exactly child's play. Death could be around just about any corner so I'd better pay heed.

At once I looked to the sky, but there were no storm warnings. Nevertheless, it would pay me to be careful. These islands had a fairly long casualty list, and it wasn't unusual to come on a shin bone or a skull washed up on shore.

24

I turned away from the gull and my thoughts went back to catching the dog. I'd have to work out some system. I couldn't just go wandering from island to island hoping to stumble on the animal. Perhaps if I put out food, a little on each island. Then, if I could get him coming to the bait, maybe I could gain his confidence. One thing for sure, if I could get him eating I would know he wasn't a ghost and I'd have a good chance of trapping him.

It would be a job putting out ten baits of food, one for each island and maybe more for Big Blue. I figured it would take at least a half-day, and then I'd have to check each bait day after day until I got the dog eating at one.

There would be no time today, that was for sure. Already the sun was getting close to the western rise of cedar trees where Eagle Point Bluff marks the mainland. Already there was a little wind cuffing the water so it kicked up in spurts which would soon turn to waves. It was turning cold so I put on my jacket and started up the incline to cross the island at its highest point and come down to the cove where I'd anchored the boat.

I was on top the rocky and almost barren little island when right at my feet something caught my eye. It was a patch of black against the sharp whiteness of stones. I knelt to it. Caught in a fissure of stone was a patch of hair — jet black hair — dog hair! I was sure of it!

I got to my feet and suddenly I had a feeling that I was being watched. I looked in every direction scanning even the beaches, but there was nothing — nothing except the white gulls soaring, a flock of goldeneye ducks flying along the surface of the lake, nothing except the bone-white branches of the dead trees and the white rock and the white, sandy stretches of beach.

I shrugged to shake off the eerie feeling and then started down to where I could see the *Killicut* bobbing gently. I was almost back to the shoreline when I first noticed Muggsy wasn't with me. I turned. She had stayed on the knoll where I'd crossed the island. I called to her, but she just sat there.

I took out the whistle to let her know I meant business, but before I could blow it she lifted her muzzle to the sky and howled. It was the most mournful howl I'd ever heard. It quavered like the cry of a timber wolf, rising higher and higher and then coming slowly down the scale until I couldn't tell if I heard her or if it was only the sound of the wind prying around among the rocks.

I was about to hit the whistle again when once more she lifted her muzzle. I had never heard her do it before — not like that. There was a tremolo to it, a ghostly and sad tremor like the wind moaning in the night. Done with howling, she put her ears at alert and looked left and right. Then she got up and came slowly down the slope to where I stood on the beach.

"What is it, Muggsy?" I asked, when she came up to me. "What's bugging you? You sound as though you smelled a ghost."

But it was over, and she was her old tail-wagging self, eager to tell me how she'd love me forever. I got back into the waders and started through the water toward the boat as she swam alongside. When we got to the boat I picked her out of the water and hoisted her aboard. I pulled myself up and standing on the deck was surprised to see the sun was gone.

I didn't like going through the cut in the dark, so I didn't bother to take off my waders. I pushed the starter, the engine caught, and after a few coughs, started purring. I put the *Killicut* into reverse and backed her slowly over the anchor. Then I put her in neutral and lifted the anchor.

By the time I came to the cut, it was almost too dark to see. My running lights didn't do much good in the half-light, but I could pick out the white stones on either side and, marking on them, I slid the *Killicut* through.

Once through I could run full throttle, but first I wanted to get out of the waders. I slipped them off and was just going into my little forward cabin to hang them up when Muggsy barked. I turned, and I got a glimpse of a big dog, only this time he was on the other side of the cut.

There was no chance now to go back. I couldn't navigate Death's Door in the darkness without risking a hole in the boat. So I gave her full throttle, and Muggsy jumped up to her blanket on the seat across from me and curled up to go to sleep.

The stars were in the sky now and in the water too. I could hear Bone Reef bell ringing. The lighthouse on Eagle Bluff was her old steady self, cutting a white ribbon across the sky every thirty seconds. In the distance I could see the lights of the village of Killicut. I knew them all — Franchot's Dock, Pappy's Eatery, Svendsen's Saloon — and in a little while I'd be able to pick out the single light at the end of my dock.

I'd tie her up and after supper I'd get to making baits. I thought how I'd get good, ripe chunks of bone and meat so they'd smell for a mile and even a ghost might come down for a bite. Of course, now that I was headed for home, I didn't really believe there was a ghost, only a big, hungry dog somehow so frightened he couldn't bring himself to come to people — a jet black dog worth three thousand dollars and the career I wanted.

3

       Next morning I towed a dinghy with a three-and-one-half-horse outboard motor clamped to her stern. After I'd maneuvered Death's Door, I anchored the *Killicut* and put off in the dinghy. It would be easier putting baits out from the little boat than having to anchor the big boat and wade ashore to each island.

I'd gotten Jens Olesen to open his meat market when I'd come in the night before, and he gave me twenty pounds of scrap meat. I had told him it was for Muggsy, and all he had said was: "Don't feed it all to her at once or she'll bust." And then he had laughed.

I turned the oven on low and, leaving the door open, put all the meat in it. I figured if it would stay warm it would rot faster, and the rottener it was, the more it would smell. It was a good, strong scent that I needed to pull that dog down to the shoreline where I'd planned on putting the baits.

I put the first offering of meat on Red Island, and I hadn't put out from shore more than a hundred yards when gulls swarmed down on it. Right there my plan went to pieces. I hadn't reckoned on the gulls. They would never let a bait alone, and I wondered why I hadn't thought of it.

I put the dinghy around and went back to the *Killicut*. There was no point in putting out the rest of the meat. The dog would never have a chance at it, or even get close enough to smell it. Already the gulls had cleaned up what I'd first put down, and now they were quarreling over the bones.

I climbed from the dinghy into the big boat and Muggsy jumped after me. I sat there trying to figure a way out of my predicament. If I was going to use the meat, I'd just have to bait one island at a time and guard it against the gulls. That would mean putting out the meat on the upwind side of the island so the scent would sweep across. Then I'd have to hide and wait and watch. It was either that or . . .

Then it hit me. Why not just screen the bait so the gulls couldn't get at it?

Lack of planning had set me back a day. It was a good lesson. I went ashore to make more thorough preparations.

Next morning I was back. All the previous day I had cut wire mesh to size and weighted the screening with lead. Now I ran the dinghy from island to island putting out baits and screening each so the gulls had no chance.

Each time I'd leave a bait, the gulls would descend in a white cloud and they'd stand looking stupidly at the screened meat and then holler as though blaming each other because they couldn't get their beaks through the wire mesh. After a while I noticed they tired of standing around and went off on patrol to find any other dead thing which might be floating on the water.

With the little boat I got the meat out on each small island by noon, and then I spent an hour putting out six baits on Big Blue. That made a total of fifteen baits to check, and I hoped to check each one at least twice a day.

I'd left the *Killicut* in the cove off Red Island and now I turned back so I could put coffee on the little stove I had in her cabin and warm myself a can of beans for lunch. After I'd eaten, I'd get back in the dinghy and make my first round of the baits.

The little outboard kicked the dinghy along at a respectable speed and I was back aboard the big boat in less than a half-hour. I'd saved a little meat from the baits for Muggsy, and we ate out on the deck.

I put off in the dinghy to check the first bait. Even before I got ashore I saw that the bait had been disturbed. The bow of the boat hardly hit and I jumped and ran to look. The wire had been pulled away and something had been eating at the meat. One bone had been dragged a good three feet.

It seemed incredible! I just couldn't believe that on my first day and at my first bait I'd get the dog eating. I gathered what was left of the meat and put it into a little pile and put the wire back over it. I went a hundred yards downwind and hid in a crevice. Muggsy squeezed in alongside, and it was warm there out of the wind with the sun glinting brightly off the white stones.

I didn't know if the dog would come back to the bait after being frightened away, but I had to take a chance on it. Either that, or I had to figure out a live trap of sorts to catch the Lab when he came to eat.

The weather was deceptively warm and pleasant for November. It was the kind of day that can lure a man out onto the big lake and then, quicker than he can get an anchor up, the wind can shift and ice and snow and bone-chilling death can sweep out of the north.

But I was watching the sky for signs, and there was nothing to worry about. It was as pale blue as the shiny side of a clam shell, and not a cloud anywhere. No wonder, I thought, that I wanted to stay in the village and be a fisherman. Where in all the world was there a more beautiful place? The lake was only a shade darker than the sky, and where they met at the horizon, the color blended together until you couldn't tell which was water.

Every island, as far as I could see, still had its gulls. They rose and fell like white confetti on the wind, and always there seemed to be a lonesome one flying its solitary way with plaintive query.

The mainland, off to the south, was a high rise of green even in winter because so many of the trees are cedars. At intervals along the shoreline naked bluffs of white limestone stood out, and if you stared at them long enough they looked like the faces of people.

No wonder Dad had loved it. No wonder he had stayed on, half killing himself to make a living when there were no fish to make a living from.

But I could remember the good days, the wonderful weeks of good fishing. They'd been few and far between even when I was small, but I never knew it. There'd been money still, and Dad had sent John, Joe, and Peter to Marquette University in Milwaukee. I'd have gone too, except I was what is called the tail ender. I came fourteen years after the others, and by the time I got to high school, mother had died and Dad was dying and the money was gone.

I never dwelt on it. My brothers would have sent me to school. I wouldn't go. I wanted to stay right here and be a fisherman. I wanted it the way it was when Dad was running six boats and the catch was so heavy the boats would be low in the water at the end of the day.

Something moved on down the beach near the bait. It surprised me so that involuntarily I moved too. My movement must have frightened whatever it was. I sat stone-still then, and I kept a hand on Muggsy's muzzle so she wouldn't sound an alarm. In about five minutes I saw movement again — something dark, almost black among the jumble of rocks.

I held my breath. Suddenly I let it go with a wheeze. It wasn't a dog, that was for sure. It was too small.

I lifted myself to peer down and saw a mink come slithering out to where the bait was. He tore at the wire with tooth and claws until he could get at the meat. Then he began dragging a bone.

I hadn't realized there might be mink on the islands. I hadn't seen any tracks, but I supposed they might swim across or walk over when winter put across a bridge of ice.

I got up and went over to the wire cage. The mink, reluctant to part with its prize, tried to stare me down. At the last instant, with a little whistle of rage, the mink scuttled off among the rocks.

First gulls and now mink! What next?

I rearranged the bait, and this time I put stones of such weight on the screening it would take an animal as powerful as the dog to get at it.

Then Muggsy and I got into the dinghy and started to make the rounds of the other baits to see if any had been disturbed. The first five baits had only gull tracks around them. At the sixth was the biggest collection of crayfish I had ever seen. They were ganged up and around and over the screening trying to get their pincers through to the meat.

I don't suppose many people know what a vicious predator the common little crayfish can be. They're a murderous little animal. Once, when one of a number of ducklings I'd been raising fell into a dry and abandoned well, I rescued it just as a whole horde of crayfish were about to charge and tear it to pieces with their big, blue pincers. The crayfish had tunneled over from a nearby creek and ganged up around the downy, yellow duckling like hyenas around a crippled and helpless antelope. I'd never have believed it.

With my foot I pushed the crayfish into a pile, killed them, and added them to the bait.

Gulls had somehow gotten the screen off the seventh bait. I had no more meat left, so Gray Island would have to go without, temporarily.

All the rest of the baits were intact, so I made a run back to the *Killicut*. On the way I got to thinking about how tomorrow I'd bring along a shotgun and some decoys to shoot ducks for bait.

The goldeneyes had been arriving in numbers. Of all the ducks they come last, riding the wind when ice starts slicking the decks. Sometimes at that time of year the water is so much warmer than the air, the lake steams like a big kettle boiling.

The goldeneye ducks are rugged as an Arctic storm and when they come high the whistling of their wings sounds even above the waves on the slabstone shores. Sometimes called whistlers, they can rocket from the sky at dawn and hit the water and be diving before a man can get a gun on them.

It seemed a shame, in a way, to use them for bait,

33

they were so beautiful, the drakes especially, with their shimmering green heads and white cheek patches. But taking a living from the lake teaches a man to accept and be thankful for nature's gifts. It's natural as picking plums. There is no other way, I thought.

Riding along in the dinghy close to the island shores I noticed how quite suddenly the wind had shifted. The weather had been too nice to last. But I rather welcomed a change. Snow would be a godsend. I could change tactics at once and start combing the islands for tracks. Give me fresh tracking snow, and if that dog was on any of the Raspberries, I'd darn soon know about it.

A real hard blow, on the other hand, would be disastrous. Although the *Killicut* was made to ride out just about anything Lake Michigan had to offer, there was always the problem of holding her at anchor. If, while I was gone off in the dinghy, the anchor should start to drag, she might go on the rocks. And then where would I have been?

I opened the throttle of the outboard wide. It was cold and I didn't have a heavy jacket along. Coming around a point on Green Island, I could see the *Killicut* riding nicely at anchor just off Red. From a distance she looked like a great white gull resting. It was only when you got closer that you noticed her planking was heavy, her beam wide, and the hull reinforced with iron to take the hammering of heavy seas and even ice.

By the time I boarded the boat I was chilled through, so before lifting anchor I heated some coffee and held the cup so the steam warmed my face. Then I drank, and I could feel the coffee go through me like electricity, warming me right down to my toes.

It was dark when I got the anchor up, so I gunned her to get to Death's Door. I wanted at least to be able to see the outline of the white shoreline so I could slip her through. If I had to go all the way around, it would take me until midnight to get off the water. The shoreline was still visible, dimly white like the milky way before complete darkness, and I swung the bow for a charge into the cut. I always gunned her through so neither the wind nor the current could sway her. It was simple, but I breathed easier doing it this way. Then I settled into my seat back of the wheel for the run to the harbor.

I had hardly settled myself when Muggsy howled. It was the same lonely, ghostly plaint she had voiced the day I found the bit of dog hair on the island. I turned my head and spoke gently, but she would not be quieted. When the lament died away she jumped from the seat and ran to the stern of the boat. I called: "Muggsy! Back, Muggsy!"

But instead of turning at the command, she jumped to the tiny stern deck just above the screw and leaped out into the night.

She was lost from sight almost instantly. Turning hard I brought the boat around. Then I slowed down lest I run her over in the dark. It was like looking for a little, black button on a blacktop road. I couldn't see anything on top of the water for more than twenty feet.

Edging the *Killicut* as close to Death's Door as I dared, I called out. I swung the boat away from the rocks to circle again. I whistled. Then I cut the engine and listened. There was nothing. I started the boat up again and thought about trying to make a run through the cut in the dark so I might anchor on the other side and make a search from land.

I brought the *Killicut* in as close to Death's Door as I dared. I got close enough to see the dim outlines of Red Island on one side and Green on the other. I turned on a small deck spotlight I used in docking, but I could not find the beach rocks with it.

Again I cut the engine to listen. There was the slap of water against the shores and the sides of the boat. I could hear the bell buoy and a startled gull. I could hear the distant and ghostly groaning of the Eagle Bluff fog horn. The *Killicut* creaked as she rolled on the waves.

I wondered what had possessed Muggsy. She had never left the boat before without being told — not even with a crippled duck swimming out front and her wanting to go more than anything.

It didn't figure, except that for the past week — or was it since we'd seen the big dog? — she had seemed what I'd call "antsy." Nights at home, instead of staying on her rug, I'd hear her get up in the night and then there'd be the click of her nails on the floor as she went to the door. I'd hear her sniffing under the door, and I had wondered what was bothering her.

It wasn't like Muggsy to be impulsive about anything. She usually deliberated, even over her food, and that for a dog is unusual. I had always been the impulsive one.

But I never had considered Muggsy a run-of-the-mill Labrador. She had a perceptiveness that was at times uncanny. She had always been considerate of others and especially of me and my wishes. She would never, for instance, race ahead through an open door like most dogs. Instead she would wait for me and then follow politely behind. Though she hated cats, she'd walk past every cat in town without batting an eye — unless it trespassed on our property. If there was a question about what she must do — as, for instance, jumping out of the boat for a duck — she'd give me a quizzical look with her ears sharply forward and her eyes watching for a sign from me.

When I suddenly felt the pull of the current where it made its run through the pass, I started the *Killicut* and ran her out and away from the rocks. Then I cut the engine and let her drift back. With regular insistence the fog horn moaned and the bell rang and the water slapped the boat. During the intervals when the horn was silent, I strained to listen until it seemed my ears were stretching out long as a mule's to get some sound of the dog.

Once there was the throb of an airplane in the sky and I saw its running lights flashing like roving stars. Once there was the splash of a fish so close that water sprayed up over the side. Several times there was the ripping of air as migrating goldeneyes cut through the night above me. And once I thought there was the rattle of stones, a noise a dog might make in running on the beach, but when I called no Muggsy came swimming to be lifted aboard.

I floated an anxious vigil until midnight, alternately listening and calling, and then finally gave up and pointed the *Killicut* toward home.

Maybe that night was the longest of my life. For the first time I was really alone. After my brothers and my folks were gone, there always had been Muggsy. And, in the nearly two years we'd been alone together, I'd taken her as much for granted as a man might his shadow. Nights, if I'd awaken, I'd lie still in bed listening for her breathing. So too on this night on awakening I would find myself listening, and then, of course, I remembered how it was that Muggsy wasn't home, that she had jumped the boat, and that all I could hope for was that she had swum in the right direction and made it to shore.

4

I was up and heading out by the first streak of dawn. Overhead the sky was flat with low scudding, gray clouds. Not bothering to make breakfast, I chewed on a peanut-butter sandwich and washed it down with hot coffee from a thermos while standing at the wheel.

Last night when I'd gotten home just after midnight, I'd found an envelope with a small check from the Smith Brothers Fisheries in payment for the chubs I had caught. So I knew that at least I would eat for a while. Bill Bratton had probably delivered it and, not finding me home, had slipped it beneath the door.

I was almost on the Raspberries when it was light enough to see well. I went directly to Death's Door and cut the engine and began shouting for Muggsy. But the waves and the bleak shore and the overcast sky threw my words back at me, so I shot through the pass and, coming around back of Red Island, anchored and went ashore.

I ran down to Death's Door. I was so anxious for some sign that Muggsy had landed. At the water's edge I began a systematic search for paw prints. Right at the edge, where the current picked up speed to make its run through the cut, I found her tracks — clear and unmistakable. I followed to where they disappeared among the jumbled rocks. Nobody could follow them on that kind of terrain.

Well, she'd landed anyway, and for that I was grateful. I combed the island from one end to the other and then decided there was nothing to do except check the baits. Nothing had touched the bait on Red Island, so I put off in the dinghy to check Green and then run on down the line to see if anything had happened at the rest.

Four baits had been raided. A mink had gotten into one, and gulls had somehow pulled the screening from the other three. But there was no sign of the dog Jet, nor of Muggsy.

I tooled back to the *Killicut*, thinking to put out some decoys to see if I couldn't shoot enough goldeneyes to bait the four islands which had been raided of meat during the night and on Gray, which had been raided yesterday.

I figured I'd carry my bran sack of wooden decoys across and hunt the opposite side of the island from the one on which the *Killicut* was anchored. A boat that big would spook the ducks and make hunting hard.

I came down to the shore, let my bag of decoys slip to the sand, and braced my shotgun against a boulder. Then I started looking for a place on the little point where I could pile up rocks to hide behind. There was a small cove just off the point and in it the water was relatively calm. Once I had decoys out, I was sure that ducks from the flocks which were crisscrossing the water would decoy in so I could kill some.

The scudding clouds had consolidated their forces to form a solid overcast. There was a stiff breeze but nothing strong enough to alarm me. So I gathered rocks and built a blind and then waded out to set the decoys. They turned every which way until the wind ran them to the end of their anchor strings, and then they swung around and floated tight at the ends of their tethers.

They were good decoys, hand hewn many years before I was born by my father. No sooner had I crouched behind the little fortresslike barricade of rocks than a big drake goldeneye broke away from a passing flock and came barreling straight in at me. I waited until I could see the white cheek patch and the glint in the golden eye, and then I lifted and, leading the duck at least eight feet to get the shot out front, squeezed the trigger. He came down like an anchor dropped out of an airplane.

When he hit the water it splashed ten feet into the air and, even though the day was dull, the spray came back down like silver rain. I walked around the rocks and waded in to retrieve him. I walked until the water was almost up to the top of my chest-high waders and still I couldn't get my hands on the drake.

I had forgotten I didn't have Muggsy along to do the retrieving and had dropped the duck too far out. The wind caught it and a wing lifted. The wing stood up like a sail and the dead duck floated farther and farther away. A cruising gull spotted it and with a cry of delight swooped down. It was followed by another and another and, even while I stood there, they ate the eyes and gobbled meat off the breast right down to the bone.

The savagery of gulls is difficult to believe unless you

know them. Most people think of them as beautiful white scavengers, peaceful birds patrolling the waterways to keep them clean. But they are without mercy, and like vultures, they often don't wait for their victims to die.

I'd have to let the ducks get in closer. The trouble was that goldeneyes don't like to come too close to shore. They are bottom feeders, and there is no reason for them to risk the dangers of a shoreline when they can dive for mollusks out where they are safe.

I walked back to the blind and crouched down to watch the passing flocks. They were really moving, and though it was difficult to discern any precise pattern, the majority of the flocks seemed to be heading south. Even above the sound of the waves running through Death's Door to my left, I could hear the whistle of their wings, an eerie weather warning saying: "Go South!"

Three hens came next. They are duller than the drakes and somewhat smaller. The three came right out of the spray thrown by the waves surging into the cut. At the angle they were flying they'd pass too far out. Then they spotted the decoys. Like a trio of fighter planes they winged over and with sizzling speed bore down on the blocks.

The maneuver was so swift and graceful it took my breath away. I leaned forward on one knee and put the muzzle of the gun up over the rocks so I could stand and shoot in one motion. When the three were over the shallows and had put down their webs to slide in for a landing, I shot. Two ducks fell, but both were only crippled and dived at once. I ran to the shore and when one surfaced I killed it on the water. The second surfaced too far out to shoot, and soon the gulls were chasing it.

I picked up the duck I had killed and then stood to watch the chase. Every time the goldeneye surfaced for air, the gulls wheeled down on it, and the duck dove. Farther and farther the helpless duck swam until the predacious birds were only a distant whirl of white above it.

It was a terrible way to die, I thought, as I turned back to the blind. But I knew it was the way for wild things. Old age was only for people. Out here where the winds rule the waters, every living thing could count on death being right around some corner.

I had one bait, and since there was no sense in hopping from island to island blindly hunting and hoping to find the dogs, I settled down to kill enough ducks so each would have a bait.

I didn't see the next flock but I heard it. The ducks came from behind and their whistling was loud over the island before I got a glimpse of the formation angling down toward the decoys. It was a large flock of maybe fifteen or twenty birds. They were high but spilling wind from their wings and dropping fast. I crouched down in the blind so they wouldn't see me, and then when they passed overhead I jumped to my feet and started shooting.

I dropped four out of that flock. They came down stone dead on the rocks at the water's edge. The rest of the birds, on hearing the three explosions of my gun, jetted straight skyward, clawing on the air to get to safety.

I had my baits. I gathered them and then went out to pick up the decoys. I cut the ducks open so the entrails were exposed and there'd be more scent. I put one on the island I'd been hunting and, getting in the dinghy, started west along the reef to put out the ducks where a mink and the gulls had raided the baits.

On Gray, fourth island west of the cut, I had just put a duck under the screening when something down the beach caught my eye. I walked over. Tracks! Dog tracks. One enormous track and a smaller one. There was no doubt about it. Muggsy and the big Labrador were traveling together.

No ghosts had left those marks in the sand. I had never believed that there was a ghost dog, but still I was relieved. The big dog lived. There was no doubt about it, and Muggsy had joined up with him.

The tracks were relatively fresh so I followed. They trailed along the beach all the way to the end of the island where they entered the water. It was obvious the dogs were island hopping, and I'd never know on which island they'd be likely to turn up. More than ever now, I had to get them feeding, coming to a bait. Once they knew there was always going to be food at a specific spot, I'd be able to intercept them, and with Muggsy along I figured the big dog might come in willingly.

I went back to the dinghy and followed the shoreline as closely as I dared. At intervals I stopped to look for tracks and to call and whistle. But there was no further sign. I put out the baits and then swung the dinghy around and putted back to where I'd seen the tracks in the sand. A rising wind had put water up on the beach and the tracks were obliterated.

Once again, for no reason that I know of, I got the eerie feeling which comes to a man on awakening from a weird dream. Had I actually seen the tracks? Of course I had. Why then did I get the feeling that I was imagining it?

Maybe the ghostly feeling was engendered by the islands themselves. I'd heard others say that they can cast a spell. I'd always laughed at such stories because, of course, I'd been raised knowing the islands the way most youngsters know their backyards. I had never seen anything mysterious about them. They were just a string of islands rising from a long, arching reef which almost shut off Killicut Bay from the bigger water.

But now that I looked around — really looked that is — it seemed I saw them in a different light. The dead trees, stripped of their bark, almost seemed to glow they were so white. If it hadn't been for the ducks and the gulls, the islands might have been separate citadels of the dead — barren, bone-white, stark, awesome. . . .

I shook the feeling and rather wished I had come prepared to spend the night. But then, what could I accomplish in the dark? I'd be helpless as a bat sealed inside a bass drum. If I left earlier and stayed until dark I would be able to utilize every moment of daylight. It was time now to go, so I went back to the *Killicut*, gunned her through the pass, and cut a white streak of water for home.

At home, under the door, was a note and it took my breath away.

"Guy," the note read, "there's a Mr. Morgan in town who wants to see you. He's staying at Mabel's place. Your friend, Bill Bratton."

If there was anybody I didn't want to see it was Morgan. I had my mind set on catching that dog myself, and now that Muggsy was living with him, I figured I had half the battle won.

I could lie to Morgan if he asked me whether I'd seen the dog. Trouble was, I'm not much of a liar. I've lied a few times and gotten away with it. But mostly when I try I can feel my neck getting hot and then I know the red is lifting up into my face and any fool would know that I was hiding something.

Of course, I could just not go to see him. I could ignore the note. There was no one forcing me to see the man. I wasn't just some dumb kid you snapped your fingers at every time you wanted him to jump. I was the *skipper* of the *Killicut* and my own man, even if the bank owned me.

I opened a can of stew and dumped it into the sauce pan and shoved it over the gas burner. Then I got out some bread and a can of mixed vegetables and a small can of pears and was just about to set everything on the table so I could sit down when there was a knock at the door.

Probably my helper, Bratton, or his buddy, Morrisson, I thought. I went to the door and opened it and had to look up, the man standing there was that tall.

I knew at once it was Morgan, because I knew everybody in Killicut and I hadn't seen this man before.

"You Mr. Hardin?" the man asked. I nodded, and he held out a hand for me to shake. "I'm Chuck Morgan," he said. I nodded again. Then he asked: "May I come in?" I had been standing there with what must have been a dumb look on my face.

"I'm sorry," I said as I recovered my wits. "Won't you please come in?" I stepped to one side and he walked past. "Have a chair. I was just going to eat. There's enough for two."

Morgan sat down. He had silvery white hair and a white mustache, and he had a face as bronze as an autumn oak leaf. His mouth was straight and firm, but it was kindly too at the corners. I liked him right then even though he was one of the last persons in the world I'd wanted to see.

"I've eaten," he said, "but if you have coffee? I can always drink coffee."

"Me too," I said. "It sure keeps a guy going sometimes." I looked up and into his eyes. They were gray.

"It sure does," he said, while I poured a cup.

Morgan sipped the coffee and then he looked at the food on the table. "You go ahead and eat," he said. "We can talk while you eat."

I sat down, and though my appetite had faded, I put some stew on my plate and took a piece of bread and started eating.

"I suppose you know about my dog," he began. I nodded. "Everybody I talk to up here insists that he must be dead, that he couldn't have survived." He paused, but I didn't say anything. He sipped more coffee and, watching me over the rim of his cup, went on: "I've been trying to get up a search party to try one last time to find him before winter ices everything over."

Then he waited for me to say something, so I asked: "Then *you* still believe he's alive?"

"Not for certain," Morgan went on, "but if he is, and there's a chance of course, then I want to get him."

I still didn't tell him that I knew the dog was alive. I knew that he had a right to know, but I also knew that I might be letting go of my one chance to get enough money to pay for the boat.

"Trouble is," Morgan went on, "the only two fishing boats working out of here are already in dry dock — not counting yours, of course. What's more, I can't even get anyone interested in searching the islands even with the three-thousand-dollar reward as an inducement."

It was no mystery to me why the men didn't want to hunt for the dog. Nobody would believe that he was alive, and every man strong and young enough to participate in the search was working either in the woods cutting pulp or down at Sturgeon Bay in the shipyards.

Norcroft, one of the men who ran one of the other fishing boats, had put it this way: "I could spend all winter looking for him, and then what would I feed my kids? The bones of that dog when I found them? I'm not looking. He's dead and my family has to eat, so I'm staying in the woods working for Messmer."

Craigston, the other boat owner, had said about the same thing. "Three thousand dollars all in one lump would be like a pile of money from heaven," he'd said, "but what is my family going to eat while I'm hopping around on those islands looking for a dog that's surely dead? How could the dog survive? What's to eat on those islands? The gulls keep it picked clean as a sidewalk. That dog won't even get to catch a crab what with the gulls being there first — unless he's big and strong enough to run a deer to death alone, and I don't believe that!"

I knew that Morgan must have heard the same thing from Craigston and Norcroft if he'd been talking to them so I didn't offer their sentiments. All I said was: "I've been looking for the dog."

He didn't seem surprised and then I discovered why. "I thought you might be," Morgan said, "because one of the men who helps out on your boat said you'd been going to the islands though you didn't have any nets left in the water."

It was time, of course, for me to tell him I'd seen the dog. He was waiting for me to say something, but I couldn't quite bring myself to tell him the truth. There was a silence in that little kitchen, and I couldn't look up at the man though I felt his eyes boring into me.

Finally the tea kettle started singing and I had to

jump to keep it from boiling over onto the flame. I set it off the heat and went back to my place at the table. I took a mouthful of stew and then, without looking up, I said softly: "Your dog is alive, Mr. Morgan. I saw him."

When I felt the man's hand on my arm I looked up into his eyes. They were bright and he was smiling. "I knew he was. I knew Jet was alive. I just knew he had to be."

I pushed my plate back and sipped coffee, and then I told him the whole story and about how my own Labrador had left me and was wandering among the islands with his dog.

I told him about the baits I had out, and how I hoped to get them both feeding at the same place so that maybe I could catch them. When I was finished he asked: "You need any help? I could bring men up from Milwaukee if you thought it might do any good."

I thought about it for a while, about a bunch of green-horn city guys running wild around those islands, and I knew they'd scare Muggsy right out of her hide, and maybe frighten Jet right out into the big lake. So I said: "If I thought a gang of guys would make a difference, I'd tell you. But it seems to me that they would only frighten the dogs and make it doubly hard to catch them."

Morgan rubbed his mustache with a forefinger. "You know," he said, "I think that's why we didn't get him in the first place. I had guys all over the islands, and I got a hunch we scared Jet right out of his wits."

"That could be," I agreed. "You take a dog that's strayed and it acts different from a dog in a kennel or at home. Where you might get a tail wag and a friendly hand lick in the kennel, that same dog is likely to turn tail and run if a stranger comes up to him while he's running free."

Morgan wanted to take me out then to buy me a beer. I had to tell him I was only eighteen, and he said he was sorry he'd mentioned it.

"I've got to get back tonight yet, but I wonder." He hesitated for a second and then said, "Could you call or write me if there's any news?"

I could laugh a little at that, because there'd be nobody happier than me to be able to call and say: "Mr. Morgan, I've got your dog!" So I said: "I'll call the minute I have anything."

He got up then and put out his big hand. I took it, and my hand, which isn't small, was buried in his. "If there's anything, anything at all that you need, just call me."

I was almost tempted right then to tell him that there was plenty. That I needed something like twelve hundred dollars and fast. That I needed some backing to get a fishing fleet ready for the day when Lake Michigan would be teeming with fishes. But I resisted the temptation. It wouldn't be any good that way. So all I said was: "I will. I'll call you if I need something."

He said good-night and went out, and I had the feeling that a sort of special man had been in my house and I didn't know why. But it was a good feeling, the kind of feeling a man doesn't get too often these days.

5

There was winter on the wind next morning. It came blasting off the big water to assault the bluff on which the village of Killicut hung. I put my head down and bucked along into it all the way to the boat. By the time I was heading out toward the islands, snow clouds were piling up in the west and I knew that before this day was over there'd be ice on the deck.

When I neared Death's Door I cut the engine and called out in the hope that Muggsy might have come back to that point at which she'd left me. But there was nothing, only the sound of the gulls and then a disturbing throb, the sound of another engine.

I started the *Killicut* up and ran her out so she'd be in no danger of going aground and then climbed to the top of the cabin for a look. A boat far out was taking off from Big Blue and heading north. She couldn't have come out of Killicut nor any harbor close by because I didn't recognize her.

A boat being out there bothered me. I wondered what they were up to. It didn't look like a fishing boat and, what's more, it was too late. It had to be someone searching for the dog.

I hadn't reckoned on any competition — not serious competition anyway. I had expected that someone might come to search for a day or two, but I didn't think anyone would make a campaign of it as I was doing.

Perhaps they had only come to look. It was a free country and I couldn't stop them. If they found Jet, I only hoped they'd catch Muggsy too, and I'd hear about it.

The nights were rough without her. I couldn't get rid of the feeling that she was in the house with me, especially when I'd awaken suddenly in the night. I'd lie there and listen and when I didn't hear her, I'd start feeling panicky and want to run right out and start searching the islands even though it was dark and I had been out there all day.

I climbed down from the cabin roof and started the *Killicut* to put her through the pass. There was so much wind that when I anchored she reared back at the end of the line and bucked like a horse. I put out a stern anchor to keep her from swinging and then climbed into the dinghy to run my line of baits.

When I came to the point at which I'd seen the boat, I crossed over and walked the beach looking for tracks. I found them all right, and I also found a bait they had put out. But it was off the ground in a leaning tree in a gull-proof latticework contraption that looked like a salt-water lobster trap.

Why in the tree out of reach? If the dog couldn't get

to the bait what was the point in putting it out? I looked northwest and the boat was barely visible. It seemed she was turning, and that might mean she was heading for Bong Bay.

I was about to turn away and head back for the dinghy when a thought struck me. I kneeled and looked closely at the sand beneath the tree. Then I took a stick and probed. There was a snap and an explosion of sand. The stick I was probing with was cleanly cut and there, uncovered, was a number-four steel trap big enough to hold a small bear.

At first I could hardly believe that anyone might try to get the dog with steel. If it didn't break his leg, it would do a good job of cutting tendons and so mutilate the leg the dog might never be able to use it.

Of course, whoever was trapping the dog could always tell Morgan he was injured when they caught him. There'd be no need to say they'd set the traps themselves.

Suddenly I was angry. My thoughts ran wild. What kind of man would set steel traps for a dog? How inhuman could man be? All the money in the world wasn't worth such deliberate cruelty. Suppose they weren't able to get back to check the traps? The dog would die a terrible death!

Because of a need to do something, I picked up the trap and, swinging it by the chain, brought it down so hard on a rock a jaw snapped loose. Maybe it was senseless, but it helped, so I kept swinging the trap against the rock until it was a piece of junk. Then I hurled it as far as I could out into the lake .

Exhausted as much from anger as exertion, I sank down on the sand. Then I started to think more clearly. If they had one trap set, they probably had others. If they did have more traps, I could look until spring and it wouldn't be likely I'd find them. There was nothing I could do and I knew it. I also knew that now luck more than anything else was going to play a big part in what happened to those two dogs.

I had to stay with my original plan. I had to keep out baits in the hope they would come to one of my eating places first. There was no other way I knew of. I had no alternative except to go along doing precisely as I had and hope that someone was looking after the interests of those dogs, just as there is supposed to be Someone taking care of the less fortunate peoples of the world.

It was a pretty flimsy sort of hope to hang onto. But what else did I have? It would take an infantry division equipped with mine detectors all winter to find any traps they might have put out.

I continued to check my baits, but the wind was so strong by now that I had to hug the shore lest the little boat capsize. Four meat caches had been raided, but none by dogs. I got back to the *Killicut* shortly after noon, wet through from the waves pounding over the gunwales of the boat. Going into the cabin I put on a change of clothes I kept there, and then taking my gun and decoys, a thermos of coffee and some sandwiches I had put up, I went ashore to shoot some ducks for bait.

I had hardly settled into the stone blind when I noticed the wind shifting, and spray from the waves running through the cut began to soak me. The anchors on the decoys weren't heavy enough to hold them in place and the blocks were beginning to wash toward shore. I looked at the sky. Something was going on up there. The clouds seemed to be milling about like wild horses getting up enough courage to crash out of a corral.

A goldeneye came in range. I shot and it fell next to the foaming edge of a curling breaker just as the last decoy rattled up among the rocks. I walked down to pick up the duck and collect the blocks. I had to lean forward to keep from being blown over.

Even as I was stuffing the decoys into the gunny sack, the wind suddenly decided on which direction it was going to push the clouds and the violent thrust with which it hit the island knocked me over and tore the breath right out of my lungs.

I dropped the bag of decoys and braced with my hands. In front of me the breakers reared in white crests and the wall of water beneath was a ghostly green. For a moment I sat fascinated at the strength of the wind and the waves. A log came riding a crest and went crashing inland only to roll back and be reclaimed by the waves.

I had never seen a tidal wave, but I had read about them. But I did know about wind tides. I had seen the waters of rivers rise four and five feet when the wind jammed water from the lake into them. Now it seemed a wind tide was about to inundate the island. One minute I had been sitting on hard rock and the next water was all around me, lifting and falling and inching me out into the lake.

I forgot about the decoys and the ducks I had killed and began to scramble toward the blind. The water was ahead of me. The rocks were awash when I stepped over them. The thermos was smashed and rattling around the inside of the blind like a seed in a gourd. My sandwiches were a speck of white hardly discernible among the foam flecks blowing ahead of the wind. My gun was underwater so I fumbled around until I felt the stock and could retrieve it. There was no sign of the box of shotgun shells I had braced in a corner.

Wrapping my arms around the gun because my fingers were getting too cold to function, I started toward the crest of the island. When I got there I could see that almost all of the island was awash. Where I stood on the knoll it was dry, but in every direction around me waves ran wild.

I started off the knoll hoping to get back to the *Killicut*. By the time I was ankle deep in water I saw the *Killicut* had been blown ahead of the wind. Her stern line had either parted or the anchor had dragged. She was shunted over to where I knew a nest of underwater boulders lay. I hoped the damage to her wasn't too great.

I looked for the dinghy. It was bobbing near the shore like a craft gone crazy. If nothing else, I had to get the little boat. Dropping the gun I ran. The wind helped by shoving me. The waves helped by lifting me. Water welled up to my armpits and I felt it slip in icy trickles down the inside of my waders to pool around my feet.

A wave caught me and threw me against the dinghy. I found the line I had tied to a root and tore it free. I braced the line over a shoulder and started back toward the island. It was like trying to pull a bucking horse. I leaned forward and though the water sometimes lifted me, I gained ground.

In the lee of the knoll which marked the island's summit there was some surcease from the wind. Sloshing around in nearly knee-deep water I loaded rocks into the boat. Finally she sank to the bottom and held. I figured the dinghy was safe, that she'd stay put. I turned to look at the *Killicut*. She was still afloat so I figured her hull was intact. I clambered up to the only dry place on the island, back up onto the knoll.

The temperature was dropping. I could feel my wet clothing begin to stiffen. I had no choice except to find some way to dry them. There were stumps, dead trees, and some driftwood on the knoll. Bracing branches and two driftwood planks between a pair of tree trunks, I fashioned a windbreak. When I had used all the available wood on the summit of the knoll, I cruised the water's edge to get what the waves were offering.

Gradually I built the semblance of a shelter. It was only about three feet high, but it was a wall against the wind and I could crouch behind it.

I'd need a fire. I collected what small wood was left on the knoll and heaped it behind the windbreak. All the while I felt myself weakening. The wind blew with terrible force. It seemed to suck at the very marrow of me. It drained me. It numbed me, and sometimes I had to lie down behind the windbreak to regain my strength.

It must have taken me an hour to get a collection of wood for a fire. Then I lay beside it and whittled splinters which I hoped would ignite and start a flame. When I had a collection of splinters I brought out what matches I had. There were ten. All looked wet. I had two shotgun shells because I usually kept some in my pocket for quick reloading.

In the tiny oasis of calm just back of the windbreak, I made a tiny tepee of splinters. Then I opened a shotgun shell and poured the powder in a heap beneath the wood. I tried a match on a rock. It crumbled. The next one I put under my cap into my hair and rubbed gently to dry it. When I struck it against a rock it flared briefly and then fizzled out.

If I got a match to flare again I hoped to ge
powder before the flame died. I took a long t
the next match. I made myself go slowly. N
more than anything could mean the difference
freezing and being warm — perhaps between liv
dying.

Finally I took the match from my hair and bn
a small stone right next to the tiny mound of powd
struck the match. It flared and when it did, I thrust it
into the powder. There was a puff of white fire as the
powder exploded. Then there was only one tiny little
thread of flame eating weakly away at a single splinter.
Once an errant gust of wind almost extinguished it, so
I cupped my hands around it. It lifted a little and put its
bright little tongue around another splinter. Quickly
then it spread until a small fire was burning. Carefully I
added wood until I had a blaze and could feel the heat,
like life itself, coming right through my waders.

After I was warm I scavenged for more wood. All that
I found had been wet by spray so I stacked it near the
fire to dry. The wood, much of it soaked with ammonia
from gull droppings, stank as it burned. But I could stand
any odor so long as it brought warmth.

Staying low and out of the wind I crawled out of
my waders. Then I stripped down to my underwear and
wrung out my shirt, pants, and socks and laid them near
the fire. I would let the underwear (I was wearing long-
ies) dry right on me.

Without the heavy waders to protect me, I froze on
the side turned away from the fire. I crowded closer
and closer to the flames until slowly the white underwear was singed and had turned brown from the heat.
But it was drying, and so were my clothes.

Maybe later, if the wind let up, I could try and make a

— get out to the *Killicut*. With the gas stove
[...]n going I would be comfortable.
[...]dreary afternoon was beginning to darken when
[...]n dressing again, and just in time. Now there was
[...]e whip of ice on the wind and the sharp sleet was
[...]ingly cold. After my clothes were back on, I heaped
[...] wood and positioned myself between the windbreak
[...]nd the fire.

At least I was warm and there was enough wood to
last for the greater part of the night. After it was gone I
could burn portions of the windbreak, and then I could
walk to keep warm.

Lying there looking into the bright fire I began to
feel sleepy. The sleet had turned to snow and now the
driving flakes seemed to fashion a cone of white around
me. The monotony of the driving snow all but hypno-
tized me as I watched the never-ending procession of
flakes. I soon fell asleep.

I awakened coughing and choking. The world around
me seemed on fire. I could smell my hair burning and
felt flames singe my cheeks. Without looking around to
see what had happened, I began to roll. I hadn't
thought about dying before, but now lying there with
the cuff of one jacket sleeve smoking it seemed a definite
possibility.

It was obvious the wind had shifted and the fire
had crept into my woodpile and then into the windbreak. With a screaming wind to fan the fire there had
been an instant inferno. Only the fact that I had rolled
without waiting to see what had happened saved me.
My waders had started to melt. I could smell the acrid
odor of burning rubber.

From where I lay I could see the fire on the knoll leap
high and the snowflakes melt into it. The windbreak

collapsed and burning embers were carried by the wind to where they were extinguished by the water. I doubt that it all took more than five minutes and then there weren't even ashes because they had mingled with the driving snow.

I got up and struggled back up onto the knoll. Even in the darkness I knew there was nothing left, not even a match. I sat down and at least the rocks were warm beneath me. I gathered those which had been beneath the fire bed so I might have a nest of heated stones to curl into. Then I lay down and, bringing my knees up to my chest, I tried to store and retain the warmth of my body against the wretched hours ahead.

I hadn't meant to sleep. I was afraid that if I did the cold might creep up on me and then, perhaps, I wouldn't awaken. But I must have at least dozed, and in a state of semiconsciousness I had a sudden and distinct feeling that I wasn't alone on the island.

I jerked awake and lay listening, but there was nothing but the sound of the wind and the water and the spit of snow. Yet I knew something was out there in the dark. I could feel it and I leaned forward as though that might help penetrate the dark. Then I heard it! A rock rolled close at hand. Instinctively my hand closed over a fist-sized stone to use as a weapon — against what, I hadn't the faintest idea.

Though I was waiting I was surprised and frightened when a dark object suddenly loomed less than an arm's length from my face. I braced to fight. Then in an instant I knew what it was. With a sad, little whine Muggsy crept into my arms and was warming my face with her tongue.

I clung to the dog and hugged her and I'm afraid there

were tears in my eyes. Never had I been so happy to see anyone.

"Muggsy, Muggsy . . ." I kept repeating, over and over.

Then suddenly it occurred to me that Jet might be with her. I sat up and strained forward again, trying to see. I whistled and called the dog by name. But if he was out there among the stones of the wind-swept island, he would not come forward.

"Where is he, Muggsy?" I asked. "Where is he?"

My little Labrador whined and turned her muzzle toward the shore from which she had come. Then she tried cuddling closer, if that was possible, and finally we settled down among the still warm rocks and, sharing our heat, we prepared to wait out the storm.

6

I think the silence awakened me. Tuned, even in my sleep, to the roar of the wind and waves and the sizzling whip of snow, I came awake with a start to a calmly quiet world. The wind, before it had blown itself out, had scoured the sky clear of clouds. The stars looked cold and brilliant as ice pellets in the black above. To the east shone a pale sliver of light. Day was dawning.

Except where Muggsy's body had come in contact with mine, I was frozen. Slowly I unwrapped myself from around the dog and tried getting to my feet. The cold, and the pounding I'd taken from the waves the day before, made every move painful.

"Muggsy, we've got to get out of here," I said to the dog.

She put out her tongue in a yawn. Then she stretched full length. When I spoke she wagged her tail.

It took me some minutes to unlimber. Light was coming swiftly to my island world and I looked about to see if the place where I'd slept was still intact. Somehow, during the storm, I had gotten the feeling that even the island would be torn to pieces and scattered by the waves.

I walked down to where the dinghy sat high and dry. She seemed in good shape. The ballast of rock had held her fast. Then I went to the shore for a look at the *Killi-cut*. She had come around and was riding peaceably right in the middle of the cove.

Walking back toward the knoll, I searched for my gun and found it about where I had dropped it. I tried to eject the shells but they were so swollen by the water they wouldn't pop out. I left them in, walked down to the dinghy, and began to unload the rocks.

I was surprised to find myself breathing heavily after lifting two rocks. I had no stamina. It occurred to me that I hadn't eaten in nearly twenty-four hours, and the ordeal of the storm and the freezing night on the cold island had taken its toll.

Resting against the gunwale of the dinghy I turned and said: "Muggsy, we aren't out of the woods yet. If we don't get out of here fast, we could still wind up as dead as a couple of frozen fish."

But if the dog had any fear she certainly didn't show it. What's more, she looked as though she'd been well fed. Being a dog, of course, she had the advantage. Dogs can take life as it is handed to them without worrying about what might happen during the next hour, the next day, or the next year. In most ways this seemed good to me, to do the necessary and hope that tomorrow would take care of itself.

Only it wasn't that simple, because I knew — I

thought — what tomorrow would bring. In fact I knew what today would bring. It was going to bring bitter, biting, ice-making cold. I knew the pattern. Now that the storm had blown itself out, the cold would follow, and it wouldn't surprise me to see temperatures well below zero before nightfall. Without matches I couldn't survive on the island. I had to get out to the *Killicut* and head for home.

When I had the rocks unloaded, I took the rope and began pulling the dinghy toward water. Muggsy grabbed a loose end and tried to help, but she only got in the way and I went to my knees.

"Okay, Muggsy," I had to laugh, though the sharp stones had bruised my knees, "that's enough of that darn foolishness." But she couldn't seem to contain herself, and with my face available, she proceeded to kiss me with her wet tongue. I had to speak sharply to get her to back off so I could get up.

At the water's edge I swung the boat about to put her afloat stern first. Then I got in and lowered the motor. I wasn't surprised when the motor started on the first pull. They are made to take a terrific beating.

Back on the *Killicut* I had the wonderful feeling of coming home. I went into the cozy, little cabin and lighted the gas stove. Within a few minutes warmth eddied up and around and into all corners. It was the most delicious feeling I could remember. The heat seemed to have substance, like a piece of soft cloth.

I opened the door a crack so I wouldn't be asphyxiated and proceeded to brew some coffee. The smell of the bubbling coffee made me ravenous. I looked into the tiny ice box but there was nothing.

But it didn't matter. The coffee, thick with sugar, was the sweetest thing ever to cross my tongue. I just sat there with both hands around the mug thinking how such little things as warmth and fragrant coffee, things we usually take for granted, can seem as important as all the wealth in the world.

Sitting there in the little cabin of the *Killicut,* even my dream of someday being president of the Killicut Crew Company lost its significance. I was alive. Muggsy was back. I was warm. I had hot coffee. These were the important things.

But, of course, I couldn't hold onto the feeling of having edged into some part of heaven. As soon as I was full of coffee and had been warmed thoroughly by heat from the little stove there was the need to proceed to the tasks before me. That is the way of life and I knew it.

My first thoughts then were of Jet. I wondered where he was and why Muggsy had left him. I could understand how she had found me. It was logical that she would come back to the place at which she had left me. Most lost and runaway dogs do precisely that. Once on the island, even with the storm raging, I knew she was capable of finding me out.

I wondered if Jet had come back with her, but at the last moment had turned and fled again? Perhaps. Dogs running wild will come only so close. They quickly learn to distrust all people and sometimes even their masters. If they are strong-minded dogs of championship character, rugged individualists, they are even more likely to try going it alone.

I went out on the deck for a look around. The air was clear and bright as fresh spring water. I could see to the far end of the island group where it curved protectingly around to shelter Killicut Bay. But I saw something else also and it startled me. I saw ice where only minutes ago I had launched the dinghy to come out to the big boat.

From past experience I knew that unless a wind came up the ice could conceivably put a hard lid right over the harbor. It wouldn't happen within an hour or even, perhaps, during this day, but by tomorrow. . . .

I had to go ashore anyway for food. Then if the wind stirred the water enough to prevent ice from forming, I could run out again to resume my search for Jet.

Thoroughly warmed I went back into the cabin and turned off the stove. After looking around to see that everything was properly stowed, I went back out and turning the key pressed the starter.

The engine was cold, but after a few false starts it caught and I let it warm up. Thinking to drag the stern anchor so I could run up over where the bow anchor lay, I put the engine in gear.

Nothing happened. I revved the engine. Still nothing happened. I put the boat in reverse. She stood still.

With a sinking feeling it dawned on me. In running up over the nest of rocks during the storm, she had broken her propeller shaft. It could happen easily, and it *had* happened, and now the *Killicut* was as helpless out there in the cove as the goldeneye which had hoped to escape the gulls.

It hit me right in the middle and the coffee I had drunk seemed to turn to acid in my stomach and I could taste it sharply on my tongue.

Hardly believing, I put the engine in gear again and let her roar as if by some miracle the shaft might mend itself and the *Killicut* would swing around and glide smoothly out of the cove to make her run on Death's Door and head for home.

Finally the futility of it hit me. I turned the key and

the silence of the icy day crowded around me and my boat. Now the islands and the lake seemed deserted. Not even any gulls hung on the air, and the ducks that had been flying before the storm had obviously found sheltered harbors elsewhere.

Muggsy, curled on her blanket on the seat, looked up at me with inquiring ears and eyes. She knew something was wrong.

"She hit the rocks, Muggsy," I said. "Hit the rocks and broke the shaft." Almost as though she understood, the dog came down off the seat and put her head against me.

Well, I had two alternatives. One was to run for shore in the dinghy and get help towing the *Killicut* to harbor, and the other was to try to pull her with that little boat and the little three-and-one-half horse motor.

Either way I couldn't take her through Death's Door. I was sure that even though she were towed on a short line there was a chance she might yaw and go aground in the pass. She would get a hole in her hull and then I'd really be up against it.

The most sensible thing to do would be to get help. Pulling the *Killicut* with the dinghy, even in calm water, would be risky. Then if a breeze should come up, the *Killicut* would probably run ahead of the smaller boat in the wind and start towing it.

Maybe this was the end of the line for me. It would be costly getting one of the two fishing boats at *Killicut* out of dry dock — so costly that I'd have to give up my boat almost at once to be able to pay the bill.

What finally decided me, however, was not the difficulties I envisioned in towing or the financial embarrassment of getting help, but the encroaching ice. Even while I'd been thinking about it, it seemed ice had been building outward from the island shore until there was already a narrow, shiny shelf.

If I didn't take her with me, tomorrow might be too late. Though the waters of the lake didn't freeze out beyond the islands, ice often did bridge the harbor all the way to shore because of the protection offered by the reef. So, the way I figured it, I had no choice. Then, if a wind came up . . . well, what if it did. Leaving the boat or getting caught in a wind, I was lost either way.

Once I'd made up my mind I lost no time. I got hold of the bow anchor line and started tugging, but the storm had wedged the hook so tightly I couldn't budge it. I went to the stern. That anchor was snagged too. The boat was fast between the pair of hooks, tied like a dog with a pair of ropes between two trees.

I wasted no effort trying to raise the anchors, but severed both lines with my knife. Then I ran a line off the bow down to the dinghy. Taking a five gallon can of mixed oil-and-gas for the outboard motor, I went over the side and Muggsy came with me.

I ran out maybe eighty feet of line and then made her fast to the stern of the dinghy. After the slack was out of the rope I revved the outboard. Slowly the bow of the *Killicut* came around. When I had her pointed for the mouth of the cove, I gave her more gas. The big boat tried to yaw to the starboard, so I turned the small boat to the port side to correct the yaw. Gradually the *Killicut* responded to the urging and then, like a tiny ant tugging at a beetle ten times its size, the dinghy dragged the big boat out to open water.

I went far enough out so if she got away there'd be no chance of her running aground. Then began the slow, cold, torturous haul around the curving crescent of the islands. There was a little current running and sometimes it turned the *Killicut*, but by countering with the dinghy, I kept her on a fairly straight course.

Once I rounded the string of islands I feared the current would give me trouble. But I couldn't think about that until the time came. Now I had to concentrate on moving steadily and in as straight a line as possible.

Once the *Killicut* had gotten up some momentum, she moved fairly easy, and by watching the shoreline of the islands slip by, I estimated we might be making a couple of knots. At that speed, with nearly eight hours of daylight, I figured we'd make dock in plenty of time.

What I hadn't reckoned on was the cold. After an hour I was shivering so uncontrollably I was making the whole dinghy shake. My right hand on the tiller of the little motor was like an icy claw, frozen fast. I knew I had to warm up or otherwise I might never make it. Loosening the line from the dinghy stern I turned the little boat back toward the *Killicut*.

Inside the cabin I lighted the stove and put on the coffee. Gradually the shivering stopped. I drank the coffee and went over the side to resume towing. Coming around under the bow of the *Killicut* to make the line fast to the dinghy, I looked to the islands and estimated I'd lost maybe an eighth of a mile by drifting out and away. But there was no other way, and twice before rounding the last island marking the long reef, I had to go aboard to warm up.

I had guessed right about the current. It was much stronger once I had cleared the islands. I had nothing to mark on now, but I guessed my speed had been cut by half.

In the distance I could see the outlines of the village of Killicut. From my position in the harbor the buildings looked like the white limestone outcroppings that marked the uninhabited portions of the shore. But, having looked at them a thousand times, I knew what each mark meant, and the sight of familiar buildings, though indistinct, gave me hope.

I also saw, far to the west, a peculiar cloud pillar which might be the nucleus of a squall in the making. If it was a wind formation and it hit me, both boats would be blown far out on open water. Then it might be days before we made land.

Finally I couldn't stand the cold and had to go aboard. While drinking coffee I stuck my head out of the door. I was surprised to see an island close at hand. The current was so strong it had drifted both boats almost all the way back to the reef. I dropped the cup on the floor and with Muggsy at my heels clambered over the side into the dinghy.

"We almost lost as much as we gained," I said to Muggsy, as I yanked on the starter rope of the outboard.

It was then I knew that it had to be all the way without a break or not at all. I couldn't afford the time to rest and be warmed. The current was too strong. So I settled my head between my shoulders and urged Muggsy to sit between my knees for warmth. *I could stay there*, I told myself. And then for emphasis I said it aloud to Muggsy: "We've got to stay here now or we'll lose the boat. We've gotta hang tough, give her everything all the rest of the way!"

Once I had said it I knew that I could do it. My watch had stopped sometime yesterday during the storm but, guessing on the sun, I gave us about two and one-half hours more of daylight. Plenty of time, I thought, as more details of the village became visible.

The peculiar cloud pillar had disappeared so I guessed that it had only been a shore smoke. Perhaps someone had used oil to burn rubbish and it had put the black cloud in the sky.

Muggsy seemed to sense I might be in trouble. She crowded close with her muzzle resting on my thigh. By alternating hands on the tiller, I could warm each against her body.

It seemed I would make it. I could pick out the roofs of the boathouses on the shore and see cars move along streets. Then we hit slush ice. It had occurred to me that the more protected waters of the harbor might freeze, but I had thought it wouldn't happen until night. But here, where there was less current, the ice had a better chance to creep out from shore and in the end it might trap me. If it did, I might just as well be back on the islands.

The boats moved steadily, however, until the slush turned to a thin skin of brittle ice. It cut our speed in half, and I knew now that the forward progress of both boats had to be maintained or we'd be trapped. I wondered how much gas was left in the outboard. I hoped it was enough to take us to the dock.

The sun dropped behind a cliff. Its last rays splintered off the ice skin which shivered with our progress. Around me night started to fall, but on shore the tops of the trees shone as brilliantly as at any noontime. It was going to be a beautifully brilliant night and already I was getting glimpses of northern lights as they shot tentative shafts upward in the darkening sky.

Quickly then the shoreline darkened, but it was never so black that I couldn't see the outlines of the trees high on the bluff and the huge bulk of the *Killicut* looming behind me.

The sturdy little outboard snarled steadily as though it had fortitude enough for us all — big boat, little boat,

70

dog, and me. The ice had thickened, but we were still moving through it and now I could clearly see the single, dim bulb at the end of my own dock.

I'd make it now, even if the outboard ran out of gas. If the motor stopped, I'd get aboard the *Killicut* and signal for help in the morning. We were far enough into the ice field that there was no danger of breaking out and floating away.

But I wanted to get in this night. My stomach was numb from not eating. All of me was cold and I had begun trembling again. Several times I tried to straighten, but I was so cramped from leaning over the tiller I couldn't get the kinks out of my back. Then, just as we were within spitting distance of the dock, the outboard quit.

Momentum carried the boats a little way and then they stopped and there was silence. I was about to get the gas can to fill the motor when I heard a voice.

"That you out there, Guy?" It was Bill Bratton.

"Yeah, it's me, Bill," I said.

Then another voice: "We were so worried." It was Natalie.

"Trouble?" Bill asked.

"Broken propeller shaft," I told him.

"Oh." Then there was a moment of quiet.

"You all right?" Natalie asked.

"Yes, I'm all right."

Then Bill asked: "You going to get through?"

"I don't think so. The outboard is out of gas, but I'm filling it."

"Maybe I can throw you a line," Bill said.

"Can you see me?" I asked.

"Not well, but well enough."

When the outboard's fuel supply had been replenished, I went to the bow of the dinghy. "Heave the line," I said. The rope came whipping past my head and I made a grab and got it. Then I made it fast to the little boat.

"When I start the engine you start pulling," I said to Bratton. Then I went back to the stern and started the outboard. At first the ice resisted, but then I heard it crack and gradually the dinghy inched past where Natalie and Bill stood on the dock. I jumped up with them, and then in minutes we had the *Killicut* alongside.

Natalie and Bill came into the house with me. I explained how the storm had trapped me, and then Natalie made a big supper. It was the first time she had been in my house. I liked it. The house needed a woman. I wondered if it would ever happen.

We all sat down together, but then suddenly I couldn't eat. I suppose the strain finally caught up with me and though I nibbled at my food I wasn't hungry enough to eat more than a few mouthfuls. While Natalie and Bill were clearing away the dishes, my head went down on my arms and I fell asleep at the table. Bill's hand on my shoulder awakened me. I looked up. The kitchen had been cleaned and was shiny.

"You'd better go to bed," Natalie said.

7

    Next morning even before I got out of bed I knew that winter had clamped an icy lid on the world. My view of the spruce trees in the yard had been cut off by a frosting of ice on my bedroom windowpane. I lighted the gas stove to warm the kitchen and, before going down to tend the furnace, looked out. Only where Watercress Creek flowed just at the end of my lot line was there open water. Scores of ducks and gulls, forced by the ice to retreat, were sporting in the creek and making the water fly. I stuck my head far enough out the kitchen door to read a thermometer on a porch post. It was twenty degrees below zero.

    Dismayed, I gave a worried shake of my head. If that big, black dog hadn't been eating regularly and was in a weakened condition, this was the kind of cold which could finish him off. Now I was doubly glad I had put out food caches and hoped he had come to one as much for his sake as for mine.

    After breakfast I was about to go hunt up Bill Bratton and Luke Morrisson to help me winch the *Killicut* out of the water when the phone rang. It was Mr. Morgan and I had to tell him that Muggsy had come back, but that I hadn't seen Jet.

Instead of being disappointed, he continued to sound hopeful. "Don't write the dog off, Guy. He's got more stuff than most men," he said.

Then I had to tell him that the *Killicut* had broken a shaft when she went aground, but that it didn't matter because the harbor was frozen anyway.

Maybe that bit of news dashed his hopes. I don't know. But, when he talked again, he sounded subdued. "Too bad," he said, "and now I suppose you'll have to abandon the search."

It was sort of a question and at once I felt sorry for him, so I said: "I think I can get out over the ice. At least I'm going to try."

He sounded concerned. "Don't do anything foolish," he said. "Don't risk your life. No dog, not even Jet, is worth that."

I couldn't quite agree with that. In my book a man should be as willing to risk his life to save a dog from suffering as he would to save a person. I suppose that sounds immature, or at least sentimental. But I know that if a barn full of horses was on fire, I'd work just as hard to save it as if the barn was full of people.

My dad had been like that. There'd been a fire in a barn. They'd gotten out all the stock except a bull which everyone was afraid to handle. I had been about eight and, hanging on top of a rail fence, watched my dad go into that burning barn. He came out with the bull. He had put a gunny sack over the animal's head, and when he pulled it off, the bull had turned on him. He barely made it to safety over the fence.

Except that my desire to get Jet off the islands, I have

to admit, was not altogether altruistic. I felt sorry for the dog. I wanted to save him from suffering. I'd do anything possible to rescue him from the predicament he had gotten himself in. But I also wanted that dog for myself. I wanted that reward. I needed that reward!

"Look, Mr. Morgan," I said, "don't worry about me. I'll be careful, but if there's a chance of getting out there I'm going. If Jet is still alive, I'm going to try and get him."

Morgan was quiet for what seemed like a long time. Then quietly, so quietly I could hardly hear him, he said: "Well, good luck, Guy, and keep me posted." Then he hung up.

I tested the ice before going for help to winch the *Killicut* into dry dock. Except for the section near the creek, it was perhaps two inches thick and I could walk on it. The creaking and cracking made me apprehensive, and I found myself trying to step lightly so I wouldn't go through.

I found Bratton and Morrisson at the Safe Harbor Inn, which meant they were out of money. Otherwise they'd have been in one of the taverns. I bought them a cup of coffee, and while we were drinking, Mattie Schofield, who was behind the counter, said to no one in particular: "I hear we've got a ghost hunter in town."

Several of Messmer's woodsmen were sitting in a booth and they laughed. Everybody in the place looked at me, and I felt my face getting red.

Then one of the men piped up: "Yeah, and by what I hear he's going to be a ghost himself one of these days if he isn't careful." There was more laughter and I wanted to tell them all to go jump, that it was none of their darn business.

There was really no meanness in their remarks. It was

only their way of having a little fun at my expense, but after having been beaten by the storm, I was in no mood for levity.

"Let's go," I said to Bratton and Morrisson, and I stalked out of the Inn. After I was outside I cooled off, and Bratton, putting a hand to my shoulder, said: "They were only kidding."

"I know," I said, "but it's no kidding matter when you darn near lose a boat."

It didn't take us long to winch the *Killicut* out of the water and swing her over into a cradle of wood I'd fashioned for her. Then I drained the engine and put a canvas over her and tied it down so she'd be protected against ice and snow.

I gave Bratton and Morrisson each a dollar from my dwindling supply of cash, and then told them I was going out over the ice to the islands.

"You're crazy," Morrisson said. "It's likely to open up any time. A little shift in the wind. A strong current. Why, you don't even know how far out the ice extends. Maybe it hasn't frozen all the way to the islands."

"I can always turn back," I said.

"If you don't go through," Bratton said.

"I won't," I said, "because I'm going to wear marsh skiis."

Marsh skiis are long and very wide. They're not made for snow, but fashioned to walk on mud, which is ordinarily so soupy it won't hold a mosquito. The skiis distribute a man's weight over a large surface, and I've walked successfully on skim ice with them without going through.

Bratton wasn't convinced. He said: "I've got a good notion to call your brother, John, and tell him what you're planning."

John was the only person who could stop me. I don't know how he'd go about it, but being my guardian, I suppose he could have the sheriff pick me up and hold me for my own protection.

"You call John," I said, turning on Bratton, "and I just might forget about being polite to my elders and punch you right in the nose."

Bratton laughed because he knew I wouldn't do it. But he knew better than to try to stop me. "Just be careful," he said. "There isn't any dog worth laying your life on the line for — not any dog, nor any fleet of boats." Bratton knew how much I wanted to get into the fishing business. He knew about my dream, but like most others, he wasn't convinced that the lake would ever produce enough fishing to justify a fleet.

"Look," I said, getting serious, "I'm taking enough stuff along so if it opens up, I can get along for awhile. Just do this for me. Check the furnace once in awhile so the water pipes don't freeze. If I'm not back in a week you can call the Coast Guard at Sturgeon Bay. Then I'll admit I'm licked and they can come take me off."

Both men looked worried, but they agreed not to raise an alarm until I'd been gone a week. Then they went off down the street and I knew they'd pop right in the first saloon they came to. I didn't begrudge them the wine they drank, the wine which made their world just a little bit rosier. Both were old fishermen. They'd seen good times and then the lake had failed them. Now they didn't have much except their wine and the conversation about how good it had been in the days when a man could pull nets loaded with fish until his arms ached. I wouldn't want to see that taken away now that their time was growing short.

Walking back into the house I debated with myself

about taking Muggsy along. In the end I decided it would be better for both of us. If I left her locked up, she'd be sad, and if I took her along she might be of some help in finding Jet — if he was still among the living.

I had my back pack ready with everything I could think of that I might need. I had waterproof containers for matches, made from empty shotgun shells waxed over with paraffin. I had a compass, rope, small axe, extra underwear, socks, and gloves. I took packages of dehydrated foods and some canned goods. I had a square of canvas for shelter and a blanket because I had no sleeping bag. One by one I put the various items into the pack trying to think if I had missed anything. When I had everything in I hefted the pack. I guess it weighed about fifty pounds, which is a lot to put on a fellow's back, especially for a long haul.

But I'm built for carrying packs. Unlike my brothers who are tall, I'm compact with a strong, solid frame and heavy shoulders. I can handle a hundred pounds on my back if it's laying right and I have a tump line to my forehead. The fifty pounds didn't worry me.

Slipping into the pack I went out the kitchen door. The skiis and a long pole were leaning against the house. I meant to carry the pole in case I went through. It would be something to lever me back out. At the ice edge I laid down the skiis and was about to step into them when I heard someone call. I turned around. It was Natalie. She came running.

Before I could say hello she started in on me: "You're a fool, Guy Hardin, for going out there to risk your life for a dog that everyone knows is dead!"

Word sure must have gotten around fast. I supposed the whole town was buzzing about it. It's like Bratton always said: "You can't blow your nose in this town without everybody knowing about it."

"I'm not risking my life, Natalie," I said. "I've taken every precaution."

"Guy, why do you want to do it?" Her entire attitude had suddenly changed and instead of sounding angry her voice sounded sad.

She knew why I had to do it. "You know," I said. "I've told you a dozen times what I want out of life. I want the *Killicut* free and clear, and if that dog is alive he's going to get her for me!"

For a moment I thought she might be going to cry so I turned away. I wasn't prepared for what she actually did do. Instead of crying she walked across the frozen grass and before I knew what she was up to she put her hands on my cheeks and kissed me right on the mouth. Then she turned and ran back toward the street.

I guess I did that first quarter-mile across the ice without ever knowing where I was. But I checked myself, because I couldn't afford such strong feelings about Natalie or any girl. I was too young, and the way things were going, I couldn't even feed myself.

The ice was holding well. I began getting accustomed to the cracking and groaning as my weight moved along. Muggsy had walked carefully at first, as though she were in a field of sand burrs and didn't want to get any between her pads. But by now she too had gotten over her wariness and was barking and racing around the shadow I made on the shiny ice.

Pushing the unwieldy skiis was wearing, so I rested and looked back. I could see the white fronts of the places on Main Street and a small crowd of people that had gathered to watch. Off to one side of the crowd, standing alone, was a figure in white, and I was sure it was Natalie.

I turned to look lakeward. There was the outline of the islands curving like a half-moon around the harbor. From across the glare ice they looked like islands in a desert mirage — lifting and falling like a reflection in uneasy water. Beyond the islands was a solid bank of fog marking the open water which was probably forty degrees warmer than the air. The fog went high, maybe ten thousand feet, like sheer mountains all covered with snow. This was the time of the year for fog and I knew it. Like wind, fog was an enemy.

After resting I continued on, holding the pole like a tightrope walker. I'd crossed plenty of thin ice in my time and I'd gone through a few times. It didn't especially frighten me. With the pole I figured I could get out. The danger lay in getting wet in freezing weather. Soaked through, a man was at the mercy of the cold.

The ice was holding well, however, and I didn't think I'd go through. I hit some rubbery spots and then the ice would give like the canvas on a trampoline, but the width and length of the skiis was adequate insurance against breakage. I guessed, as I shuffled along, that I might be able to walk on a film of oil. Of course I knew I couldn't, but it seemed that way.

Next time I looked back the village was only a blur of white among the cedars which rose from the bluff, but out ahead the islands were coming into focus and I could make out Death's Door between Red and Green. I figured to head for the pass and start my search from there. Though the fierce winds had swept the islands fairly clean of snow, there were pockets of white where I might locate tracks. I guessed I could get from island to island by walking over the ice on the mainland side of the chain. I knew the waters would be open on the lake side.

While I stood there a whisk of wind whipped sharply across my cheeks. I didn't like that. Wind could shift the ice and open cuts. Eventually they would close again, but stretches of open water would delay me or even make me turn back.

I hurried a little hoping to make land before the wind picked up. Muggsy seemed to sense the change in the weather and came in closer. Several times I had to scold her for stepping on the trailing ends of the skiis. I couldn't afford to fall. A fall might break the ice.

I was tiring. The pack, which had felt like next to nothing when I strapped it on, seemed now to be weighing me down. I bent forward and shuffled along with my eyes riveted on the tips of my skiis. I must have walked for fifteen minutes without looking up. When I did raise my head I was surprised to see that the islands had disappeared.

At first I couldn't believe what my eyes were telling me. I had been so close I was already marking on certain trees and rocks. Now where the curving bow of the islands had been there was nothing. It startled me so that I stopped abruptly and rubbed a hand over my eyes thinking perhaps the glare of the sun on the ice had impaired my vision.

But my eyes were all right, because I could plainly see Muggsy, and when I turned I could still make out the white outlines of village streets.

Then it hit me. The wind had moved the fog bank across the islands. They were swallowed in the dense mist. Shortly now the fog would swallow me!

8

The mist moved like a solid wall of white. Standing there on the ice I got the feeling that it might crush me. Sun shining on the dense clouds cast back a vivid reflection. Then I felt it touching me with wet fingers. Muggsy whined and I felt her head against my knee. I waited to be swallowed up, immersed. When it happened it was an eerie experience.

I don't know how long I stood there with the white cloud bank wrapping itself around me. I only knew that my mind was running the gamut of stories I had heard about men who had wandered for days on the ice without breaking out of the fog to find shore.

It had never occurred to me that I might be frightened by fog. I had a compass. I could see far enough ahead to keep from walking off the ice into an open cut of water. I had provisions and I couldn't be more than a half-mile from the island chain. Yet I couldn't orient myself. I couldn't make myself move forward.

It was as though I were a child again and had awakened in a dark bedroom to have the chairs and dresser take on weird and ghostly shapes. I tried to shake the childish feeling by talking to Muggsy, but my voice echoed in the fog bank and came back to me like the voice of a stranger.

A flock of ducks must have passed overhead, but instead of ripping the air with a sharp whistling, they went on with a swift, soft sigh. I looked down. The fog eddied like smoke around my feet. It curled over the upending tips of the skiis. It fingered down around Muggsy giving her shiny, black coat a misty sheen. It seemed I could almost feel it reaching under my collar and down my neck, into my pockets, up my nostrils, like some living thing intent on consuming me, making me a part of itself — a part of the fog.

Then suddenly I was ashamed of myself. "Like a fool kid in a cemetery," I said aloud, and the echo came back to me: "Like a fool kid . . ." but the last three words were indistinct.

This would never do. I put a hand to Muggsy's back just to reassure myself that she was real, that I was real and alive and the cottony clouds around me were, after all, nothing but fog. I got out my compass and made myself take a bearing. Then I started walking, and Muggsy went on ahead a little as though to scout out the way. Sometimes the fog would roll in so thick her legs would disappear and she would look as though she were swimming in milk.

The sound of my skiis skidding along over the ice was an enormous scratching as of sandpaper against sandpaper. Even when I cleared my throat, the small sound startled me. But I kept walking on and on, and there was no land. I stopped and took out the compass. I was surprised to note that I had veered sharply to the right and was walking almost parallel to the islands instead of toward them. It made sense. While still a kid I had broken my right leg and ever since my left leg had been stronger. In skiing I was pushing harder on the left and swinging right.

I corrected my course, and now I kept the compass in my mittened hand so I could refer to it constantly.

Gradually the eerie feeling began to leave. As I became mentally acclimated to the fog, the dampness which had seemed to bore right through the marrow of my bones became bearable. I was back in control, and as I walked, I resolved never to let my imagination get the upper hand again. I knew from experience, and from the many stories I had heard, that a vivid imagination can be the mother of panic, and I knew that when a man panicked he could get himself killed.

Boulders jutting right up through the ice were the first sign that I was approaching shore. Around each boulder was a narrow ring of open water indicating that the stone was still warm. I had to stay away from them, but I couldn't help hurrying and Muggsy, obviously scenting land, ran on ahead and disappeared.

Then the rocky beach came in focus and in seconds my skiis were clattering over the stones. I got out of them, and it was like finding my feet again after floating on a cloud.

Muggsy was as happy to be off the ice as I was. She barked her joy and skittered back and forth and in circles like a young pup just let out of the house.

I carried the skiis and climbed the sloping shore until I came to a flat rock where I decided to camp. I had no idea on which one of the ten islands I had landed, but guessed I couldn't have wandered too far away from

Death's Door. It was a relief to shake out of the back pack. After stretching my arms and moving my shoulders back and forth to get the circulation stirring where the pack straps had cut in, I gathered wood for a fire.

The fire, more than anything, dissipated the last shreds of gloom and my uneasiness went with them. The flames leaped into the air and I could not help but re-reflect on how the man who first found fire must have felt.

Nevertheless I was alone on an island, and being alone on an island in a fog is like being alone in the world. I'd have to keep busy, and since there was no point in looking for the dog in the heavy fog, I thought to make this tiny universe of mine a little like home by establishing a base camp.

Around the six-foot square rock slab on which I'd dropped my pack I built a low stone wall, leaving only a narrow gap for an entrance. When the wall of stone had risen several feet, I covered it with the canvas I had brought, weighting the ends and making it taut with other stones.

There, I had a house! There was room to lie in it comfortably so I spread my blanket. There, I had a bed! Here was protection from wind, ice, and snow. I might, if it became necessary, even heat rocks in my outside fireplace and roll them into the house to warm it. There, I had a heating system!

But I wasn't out on the islands to play house, so when I'd lunched on a small piece of chocolate and a handful of raisins, I went to the north shore to follow along the open water and find, if I could, the meat cache I had put on the island.

In the fog I recognized no landmarks. I might as well have been on the moon, it was that strange. But then, all the smaller islands looked alike. Although I did find where the meat had been cached, now there was only a scattering of bones and I couldn't determine whether dog or gull or mink or some other meat eater had come raiding.

Muggsy sniffed enthusiastically along the ground where the bones had been scattered. If she could have talked, I'd have known what bird or animal had eaten the meat.

"Muggsy, what was it?" I asked. "Gulls? Another dog?" But, of course, though Muggsy had the answer, she couldn't give it to me, and I think I talked to her only to dispel my own loneliness.

I walked the island all the way to the end. Not having brought the skiis I didn't risk the ice to cross over to the next island. I turned back.

There seemed little chance of accomplishing anything in the fog, so I went back to camp. I busied myself collecting firewood and my small axe rang out, a brave sound on the ghostly fog-bound island, as I felled small trees. All day the cold hadn't bothered me, but now that I stopped moving about, I could feel it, like an invisible force pressing through my clothing against my skin. I rolled a half-dozen large rocks into the fire and built it up.

Any qualms I might have had about survival were gone, but now I wondered if I wasn't perhaps making a fool of myself camping out like this to conduct a search for a dog that might be dead. Of course, I couldn't let myself believe Jet was dead. It was absolutely necessary that I keep my faith in the belief that he was alive.

I'm not quite sure when night came to the island. In the fog it seemed there could be no daylight or dark, but only a gray in-between time as marks dawn or dusk. Then quite suddenly a wind sprang up and the fog bank lifted. High above, the stars were bright between horse-tail clouds which were being whipped around by the same wind which had carried off the fog.

It was a good sign. With a wind like that the following day would most likely be clear. I let my fire burn down so I could set a can of beans into the coals. Careful not to let them get hot enough to blow sky-high, I retrieved the can after fifteen minutes and, wearing mittens, pierced the cover with my hunting knife. When the fragrant steam escaped with a hiss, I cut the can open.

I can eat beans three times a day and every day of the week. I think they are the finest of foods for the trail, because if they've been dried they weigh next to nothing, but can give a man all the energy he needs.

While the beans were cooling, I mixed flour, water, and salt in a small kettle. Then winding the dough around a stick, I baked it until it was brown. It was such a fine feast I was tempted to do it over again, but instead I settled for a small piece of chocolate and a couple dozen raisins.

I sat with my back to the stone house and while I watched, the northern lights began building in the sky. They have always fascinated me, though I've never found words to describe them. Once I tried describing them to Natalie, but the most I could say was that they looked like shafts of purple marble — liquid marble spouting like a fountain — and then as they crested overhead, the marble shattered and spilled away down the sky turning to many colors as it fell.

I sat there a long time looking into the fire, and mostly I wondered if I'd ever see my dreams come true. And I wondered too, if someday I might marry Natalie or if what I felt for her was the usual kid stuff adults are always laughing about.

87

I couldn't help, of course, wondering about Jet and if he were alive, because at this moment his capture would open the first of the doors to my future.

Gradually my dreams slipped into things past, and I remembered how it was when my father and mother were living and my most pressing problem was could I get out of work on Saturday to play baseball with the kids. Sitting out there alone on the island those days seemed a hundred years gone.

I shook myself and stood up. Muggsy got up too and stretched. I could feel the cold settling in so I pulled the rocks out of the ashes and rolled them into my stone house. They were so hot that when I spit on one it sizzled. When they were arranged along either wall, I crawled in and curled up in the blanket. Muggsy availed herself of a small place I had left for her and with body heat from the both of us and from the stones, the rock house warmed and we slept.

Maybe it was midnight or after when Muggsy growled. I came awake and lay listening. The growl subsided to a whimper. I whispered: "Muggsy, what is it?"

She crawled to the narrow opening and went out. I unrolled from the blanket and followed. A half-moon had risen while we'd slept and it helped to light up the island. Muggsy was down along the beach and I ran to her.

I stood on the shore and looked in both directions but could see nothing. Finally Muggsy came to me, and then I got to my knees to look for some sign in the sand. I crawled along where Muggsy had been sniffing and there was the track, the track of a huge dog.

I got to my feet and called out: "Jet! Jet! Here, boy. Here!" But my words only started up some gulls that must have been roosting on the shore. I ran in the direction the tracks were headed and as I ran I kept calling. When I came to the end of the island I knew the dog had gone, and then it was I realized I was running around in the cold night in my shirt sleeves and my stocking feet.

Shivering I went back to the rock house and threw some wood on the still-hot ashes. When flames began licking up through the wood I crawled inside to get my boots, jacket, cap, and mittens. I put more wood on the fire until flames were leaping and I was warm. I put on my clothes and with Muggsy began a tour of the island.

Judging from the distance I had walked to get from one end of the island to the other, I guessed I was on Gray. The light from the moon whitened the rocks and the trunks of the trees which had been stripped of their bark because of the seagull occupancy. The tree trunks and the limbs were skeletal, like the reaching bones of dead hands.

I walked around the island a half-dozen times, but there was nothing. Then I went back to the fire and built it up. I didn't feel that I could sleep again although it was only two thirty. So I sat looking into the fire and Muggsy lay down beside me. Together we waited, hoping the big dog would come back, hoping that the warmth of our fire, the need for companionship — something — would bring him to us.

I could only guess, of course, why he disdained human companionship, why he had taken to running wild. It was my guess that in his veins, as often happens, still lived the primitive need to be a completely independent animal — a wild dog, like the countless generations of wolves and wild dogs before him.

I knew from reading that living things have been domesticated for only a tiny fraction of their time on Earth. For millions of years dogs ran wild. They came to camp with man only a short time ago.

Muggsy was uneasy. She left the fireside frequently to circle the area and to stand looking off into the distance. "What's gotten into you, Muggsy?" I asked. "Is that big dog out there somewhere?" She looked at me the way all dogs do when they are trying to make you understand.

Several times I got up and went with her beyond the circle of firelight and down to both beaches. On one side, of course, the lake was frozen but on the other the waves still rolled. Once again I walked all the way to the end of the island and called, but there was no answering bark and the big dog did not come out of the night to show himself.

I went back and built up the fire again and tried to call Muggsy close so we could share each other's warmth. She wouldn't come near, but sat outside the circle of light watching. Then quite suddenly she raised her muzzle and howled in the forlorn way she had previously. It was a primitive plaint adding to the ghostliness of our surroundings. Then when the howl died away on a thin, wailing note, she sat with her ears alerted to catch any sound and turned her head from side to side.

I thought I heard an answer. It came from such a great distance that perhaps I heard nothing at all, or maybe it was only the wind prying around among the moonlighted rocks. But Muggsy cried so deep down inside herself that I could barely hear it. It was a sound of such yearning that I suddenly realized my black dog wanted to be with Jet, and only her faithfulness was keeping her by my side.

90

Why hadn't I understood before? What was there about people that made them so insensitive to the needs of animals? Were people so selfishly concerned with their own well-being that they failed to understand even the simplest and most primitive needs of the dog?

And here all along I had thought I knew Muggsy. We'd been together constantly during the five years of her life and yet I perhaps had only half-understood her deepest needs.

In a wave of remorse I tried calling her to me so I might reassure her of my continuing affection, but she would not come. At this moment she did not want me. She wanted the dog Jet, and if I hadn't been her master, I'm sure she would have gone directly to him.

Only the approach of daylight could shake my mood of depression. With the sun sending silver signals into a low-lying ridge of clouds, I cast off the dreamlike feelings of being all alone in another world with two dogs, both of which had suddenly become strangers to me.

Muggsy seemed to shake herself back into my world again. She crowded close to get some bacon strips from the slab I was slicing. I mixed another batch of dough for stick bread, and we breakfasted together.

When we'd eaten, I put all of my gear except the skiis and the long pole and a length of rope into the rock house. Then shouldering skiis I went with Muggsy to the far end of what I now knew was Gray Island.

The bright, brisk day invigorated me, and the eerie feeling of the night before disappeared as had the mist. I was strong again, strong and confident and I thought: "Maybe this is the day! Maybe today I'll catch the dog."

9

It was noon, and, upon looking up, I saw a large boat cutting around the ice field, apparently to make a landing. I had traversed all the islands out to Big Blue and had come to the conclusion that running down the big dog was an impossible task. The size of Blue, largest of the island chain, is what discouraged me. It is heavily wooded. There are small swamps in the interior and two small lakes. There are little hills and sharply deep valleys in between. The island is for all the world like a piece of the mainland which has broken away and floated out here into the lake.

At intervals on the smaller islands I had come across the dog's tracks. It was obvious he was headed for Blue, and I felt that he had to be on the island. But it was conceivable that I might hunt for years without even getting another look at him.

I wondered what the boat was doing on the lake and from what harbor she had come. She looked like the same boat I had seen on the day I discovered someone was setting traps for the dog.

The long morning had tired me and Muggsy was limping a little so I stopped to examine her paw. She had cut a pad on a sharp stone, but it was nothing serious.

I looked back out at the boat. If she was headed for Blue it would be a half-hour yet before she arrived, so I continued my search.

Mostly I stayed to the beach. Tracks in the sand might offer clues. Inland there were drifts of snow, but nowhere was the covering adequate for tracking. Blue has a wide beach of sand and only at intervals do rocks come all the way down to the water. These infrequent rocky shores, some having large boulders, are on the points which jut out into the lake and can be swept by wind and water.

I was thinking what a beautiful island it would be to live on when I came around one of the rocky points and something back among the trees caught my attention. I swung inland.

It was a deer, a dead deer. Muggsy ran ahead and began sniffing the carcass. When I came up I saw at once that it hadn't died a natural death but had been run down and killed. The doe's throat had been torn open and something had been eating at the vitals.

I dropped to my hands and knees to examine the ground around it. It was an old kill and signs were faint. Since dying, the body had been visited by whiskey jacks, and there were mink and weasel and what looked like fox tracks. Then, off to one side, I found a single large dog track and on a wait-a-bit bush there was a tuft of black hair.

There was only one animal on the island with hair as jet black as that. The evidence was strong against the dog, for I couldn't think of any other island animal that would have the strength and speed to run down and kill a mature whitetail deer.

I wasn't really too surprised. The corpse explained a lot of things. I knew now why the dog hadn't come to the baits I had put out. I knew too why he hadn't come when I called and why he hadn't sought the safety and the comfort of our camp fire.

Jet had obviously heard the primitive call of all his wild ancestors. Once the blood of his victim had come gushing warmly over his flews and across his tongue, he obviously had followed his wild inclinations. It happens too often in deer country. The nice conventions of civilization and all its comforts hold no allure when the dog knows about the wild call to kill. Sometimes dogs gang up and run like wolf packs and then there is no way except to hunt them to their deaths. Sometimes men retrieve their dogs and bring them back to the hearth, but never afterward do they dare take the animals into deer country unless they are on leash.

Jet obviously had turned outlaw. At least that is what they would say about him, though I thought it was badly put. The word "outlaw" infers that whoever is so described is operating outside the law. Actually Jet was operating within the law, the law of his kind. Dogs have nothing to do with laws which say thou shalt not kill. I wondered why people didn't realize this. In the beginning, and during every age since the dawn of time, they have been killers. It is only during the relatively short time that man has fed the wild dog that he has not been forced to kill.

I was almost certain that I now knew who manned the boat which had turned and was approaching the island. Aboard would be conservation wardens and their aides. Big Blue was a game refuge. It was inspected regularly. They would know that the dog was killing off the island's deer, and Wisconsin law said emphatically that any dog running deer must be shot on sight.

It was these men then who had set the traps. Cruel as steel traps might seem, I knew the wardens were within their rights. I knew too that a dog as big as Jet could literally wipe out the deer herd on Blue Island once the snow got deep. Many lesser dogs could run a deer to utter exhaustion in deep drifts. And Jet would keep on killing and killing and killing for the pure joy of it.

With the sure knowledge that Jet was a killer, my hopes for collecting the reward began to fade. If the conservation department wardens were having trouble catching the dog, what chance would I have?

The boat had swung into a cove. I could see she was named the *Aldo Leopold* after the state's father of conservation, the man who many years ago had formulated the ground rules for the preservation of natural resources. There were at least a dozen men aboard and they began coming ashore in dinghys they had been towing. All were carrying rifles.

The sight of the guns jarred me. I quickly called Muggsy to my side and put the rope I was carrying around her neck. I was afraid she might run out onto the beach. If she did, they'd surely shoot her by mistake.

When the first boat landed I went down to the beach with Muggsy trailing behind. All the men looked surprised. The one who first stepped ashore said: "Don't tell me you've caught the devil!"

"No," I hurriedly explained. "This is my dog. The one you're looking for is still on the island."

The man came over and said his name was John Helsing. I knew the name. He was supervising warden for the area, and leader of the posse. I held out my hand and introduced myself.

"Where's your boat?" Helsing asked.

I told him I had crossed over on the ice from Killicut.

"What in the world are you doing out here?" he asked.

I told him I was looking for the dog too. "I made camp on Gray," I explained, "and I was hoping to catch the dog for the reward money."

"You'll never catch him in a million years," Helsing said.

I told him that I knew now that I couldn't, but that I hadn't known Jet was killing deer.

"We've counted six carcasses already," Helsing said, "so you can imagine how many there would be by spring."

"It's too bad," I said, "because he's a champion."

"We know all about him," Helsing said, "but if you're going to talk money we have no choice. We figure deer are easily worth a couple hundred dollars a head, so champion or no champion . . ." Then he must have noticed that I was pretty down in the mouth about the whole business, and he lowered his voice: "I'm really sorry. We'd much rather not, you know. But the law is the law, and you know that in time that dog can do more harm than a pack of wolves. At least the wolves will quit killing when their bellies are full."

The other men had come ashore and were grouped around us. Helsing explained about me and how I'd been trying to catch the dog. Then he turned to me. "We could use your help," he said. "We're going to drive the island and try to force him out on a beach so we can shoot him."

I didn't think I could bring myself to help drive so the dog would be forced into the sight of a gun. I looked at the men around me. They seemed to be waiting for my answer.

"You don't have to, of course," Helsing said, "even though I have the right to insist that you do."

I looked at the men again. I supposed if they wanted to make me hunt Jet they could. I knew they had the power to enlist men to fight forest fires or deputize them during a manhunt, so I assumed Helsing would be within his rights if he drafted me now.

I looked around at the men again. There were a couple of boys among them. At least they weren't quite men. About my age maybe, eighteen or a little older.

"I don't suppose there is any other way?" I made it a question, even though I knew there was no other way, otherwise they would not have come with guns.

Helsing shrugged. "We've had live traps and steel traps out. He won't come to a bait. There is no other way except to put out strychnine, and poison would endanger the lives of too many other animals. He probably wouldn't pick it up anyway."

I hated to give up. "Perhaps we might surround him, run him into a fish net, or build a corral and corner him into it."

I could see that Helsing was becoming impatient with me. "You know as well as I that we'd never get close enough to get a net over him, and by the time we got around to building a corral, winter would be on us."

All that he said was true. There was no other way, but

it was hard to concede that I had been defeated. Helsing had turned to his men. "Let's take a last look at the map," he said, taking a scroll from a little packet strapped to his belt. He spread the homemade map of the island on the sand and the men grouped around.

"Matt, you start here," he pointed to a check mark, "and you walk straight east and come out here." He pointed to another check mark. "Burt, this is where you take off from." He looked around and then said: "Mack?" A boy stepped forward. "You swing the end of the island, Mack, because you're faster and can cover more ground. Jim . . ." Another man stepped forward, and then to each in turn he pointed out what amounted to their battle stations.

When he had reviewed the assignments he turned to me. "Well?" he asked.

"Okay, I'll go," I said.

"Fine, but I think you'd better take your dog out to the boat so she doesn't get shot by mistake. You'll find an extra .30-30 rifle in the cabin. There's ammo on the shelf."

The young man named Mack helped me row out to the *Aldo Leopold*. On the beach the men sat talking and smoking. I locked Muggsy in the cabin and took the little carbine and a handful of shells. When we got back to shore Helsing said he wanted me to be an end man "because you're young and you look tough."

The men started to move out even before Helsing said: "Now everybody to your positions. I'll give you fifteen minutes and then when you hear me shoot start driving and make lots of noise so the dog will run ahead of us."

The little gun balanced nicely in my hands. It felt good. I like guns. They are precision instruments. But unlike most instruments, the gun depends to the utmost in cooperation from the man who is using it. That's why I like them.

I swung down the beach toward the end of the island, and though I was acutely aware of the logic which had brought these men out to kill the dog, my sympathies were with Jet. I hoped he would somehow get away.

I had killed a dog once, and at the time I had vowed never to do it again. Three years ago a neighbor brought me his little fox terrier. He had been so crippled by age that he couldn't walk or eat and the only way he could take water was from a damp cloth.

"Please shoot Solomon," the woman had begged, and when I had seen the tears in her eyes I had agreed. There was no humane society or any veterinarian to take the dog to. So that was the way all sick and aged dogs had to be put out of their misery — by shooting them.

I'd taken the fox terrier into the country and dug a small grave and put the dog into it. There he sat, and only his big brown eyes kept begging me not to shoot him, but I did and I was sick for a week.

Of course, there is such a thing as measuring up, and it becomes a man's lot to do some unpleasant things regardless of personal feelings. No one could have doubted that Solomon was better off dead than alive. He was miserable. But to shoot him? Yet, how else? And if I hadn't done the job there would have been another and maybe that someone else wouldn't have made it as swift and neat and clean.

I came to my position at the end of the island and leaned against a boulder. My watch said there would be a wait of three minutes before Helsing gave the signal. Standing there I wondered if I would be capable of killing the dog. If Jet broke clear of cover in my area could I bring the gun up, pull the trigger? What would I say to Morgan? Would I call him and say: "I just shot your dog!"

My thoughts were broken off by the blast of the gun. There was a single echo as the sound slapped against the woods and then recoiled to go rolling back and away across the flat water. All up and down the beach then there were sounds of shouting as the men moved in, trying to create enough of a disturbance to make the dog run ahead of them.

I'd never driven a dog before so I had no idea how it would work. I'd been on many a deer drive. I knew whitetails would run ahead of a noise. But I also knew that if there was a clearing such as an open beach ahead, deer would not go out onto it. The animals would turn back before coming clear of cover and try to sneak through the line of hunters.

I was sure the wardens and their aides knew this too. They were all woodsmen. I was sure they had used a battle plan such as this before. They would be alerted for just such a maneuver on the part of the dog, and if he tried it, they'd likely get him anyway.

I took out my compass and took a reading so once I was in the brush I wouldn't get turned around and circle back. Then I let out a yell and stepped off the rocks onto the yielding ground of the forest, into the brush among the big trees.

The hunt was on.

10

I hadn't taken ten steps into the forest when I heard a piercing howl. I stopped, startled, and it took me a few seconds to realize that the howling was coming from the boat anchored in the cove. It was Muggsy crying out, but how could she have known what we were about to do?

Yet, she must have, and I believe she did know. I've had enough experience with dogs and other animals to understand that they can often intuitively know a person's intent — either that, or they can smell it through some strange chemical change in the human body.

I kept walking, but I thought about how animals know more about what we humans plan on doing than we generally give them credit for. I knew then and I know now that the little fox terrier was aware of my intentions to kill it. It was plain to see in the dog's eyes.

Though it was cold, the sound of Muggsy's howling had me sweating. I wondered if she had been singing some sort of funeral dirge or if her howl was meant to warn Jet. Or if, in reality, it was only a howl of loneliness and I had just been reading too much into the whole affair.

I stood for a minute and then realized that I was falling behind and not keeping up my end of the drive. I could tell from the shouting that the others were in a line out ahead of me, so I shoved along through the brush and started shouting so if Jet were out in front of me he'd head for the opposite beach.

Helsing had wanted me to swing a half-circle to take in the long point of the island. I took out my compass to make sure I was on course. I was probably halfway across when a sound in the brush ahead alerted me. I dropped to one knee and got my rifle up and ready.

Visibility was cut to perhaps thirty feet by hazel brush. Whatever was out there was being careful not to make noise. Sometimes I could hear it, and then there would be nothing.

Don't let it be Jet, I said to myself. Don't put me to the test, I pleaded with whoever is in charge of the course of events. I still didn't know if I could bring myself to shoot the dog, and I would rather that I wasn't given the chance to find out.

I must have been holding my breath in anticipation because when a fawn stepped into a small clearing I let it go with a hoarse whistle. The sound alerted the fawn and it jumped and disappeared. As I was about to get to my feet, a doe bounded past me on the trail of the fawn. I started to walk and there was a crash in the brush. A tremendous buck came vaulting past so close I could almost reach out to touch it with my gun barrel.

It was obvious the deer were filtering back through the line of drivers and would probably go all the way to the edge of the timber, to the fringe of beach from where we had started the push.

After I got my breath back I started driving again. Once I got a glimpse of a tawny flash of fur and thought it might be a fox. A few snowshoe hares, mottled brown and white because of the changing seasons, hurried to get out of the way. From on high I could hear seagulls screaming at the intrusion, and closer, among the trees, chickadees and downy and hairy woodpeckers moved nervously among the branches.

I estimated I was three-quarters of the way across when with a crashing of sound there came a shot. It seemed so loud on the island that I could have believed that the air about me shivered. I stopped and, holding my breath, listened again. All the shouting had ceased. Even the little birds sat still and silent.

Of course, it was supposed to end like this, and though I had fully anticipated it would, I felt I had suddenly lost a long and arduous fight. With the feeling of loss, I also experienced a feeling of weariness, as though I'd actually been in physical combat for days and days and had finally been beaten down.

I had to sit on a log to recover. When I was breathing normally again I got up and began hurrying toward the beach. The little birds around me were busy again, but the sound of shouting didn't start up. It took me about ten minutes and then I broke out on the ice-bound side of the island.

I could see several men down the beach a ways and I started toward them. The shot had put up the gulls and they looked like white umbrellas over the lesser islands on down the line.

When I got to the three men a fourth was coming out of the brush to join them. None of them had fired the shot, nor did they know who had. One by one then, the men came to the open beach and walked over to join us. Helsing came last, and it was he who had shot.

"I missed," he said. "Missed clean." I suddenly felt relieved. Jet still lived. Then Helsing explained: "He's smart. He's awful smart. He knows we're out to get him. He wouldn't come down to the beach but was trying to cut back. He was going low and fast like a wolf that knows it's running the gauntlet."

Some of the fellows started kidding him about his marksmanship, but Helsing didn't laugh. I thought he seemed almost glad that he had missed, or maybe I only thought he gave that impression. But I wouldn't have been surprised. Most wardens hate killing dogs, though they have to do it. Some even hate killing rampaging bears or even egg-robbing skunks. But if I thought Helsing might abandon the hunt because one drive had failed, I was dead wrong.

"We'll rest and try again," Helsing said. "And we'll keep on trying, and if we can't kill him on Blue maybe we can drive him over to one of the smaller islands where we'll have a better chance."

Some of the men smoked while others ate sandwiches they had stuffed into their pockets. Helsing came over to me. "You got anything to eat?" he asked.

"My food is back on Gray," I told him. "I didn't bring anything along."

He took a sandwich from his pocket and gave me half. I didn't know how hungry I was until I started eating. After I'd eaten, another of the men came over and offered me a cigarette. I thanked him, but said I didn't smoke because I couldn't afford expensive habits. He laughed.

When they had rested and drunk from the canteens they had dangling from their sides, they gathered in a circle with Helsing in the middle. He waited and looked around as though to give them time to say anything they might be wanting to say. Then he directed: "We'll drive again, only this time we'll push toward the open water." He waited again as though for suggestions. When no one spoke up, he continued: "I don't know how many of you have noticed, but I'd guess the temperature has dropped maybe ten degrees in the last half-hour. There's weather in the making." He turned and pointed. For the first time I saw the enormous fog bank far out over the open water.

Helsing cleared his throat and said: "I doubt if we'll be able to make more than one more drive today. So let's make it good. Let's get him. If we have to come back it will be with shotguns loaded with buckshot. If I'd had a shotgun today, we'd have him now!"

I knew most of the men didn't like using shotguns. There was too much chance of only wounding an animal with one or two pellets. All good hunters preferred the rifle because, if they were on target, that was it — death in an instant.

"Take the positions on the beach where you came out," he said, "and then when you hear the signal, follow along on the same course you took coming over."

The men strung out then, and I went back to where I'd come out of the trees onto the stony beach. I was shivering now. Bucking the brush had been sweaty work, and now, as I stood on the windy beach with the temperature dropping, my damp clothing felt icy against my skin. I was anxious to get moving, if only so I could be warm again.

The sound of the signal gun put the gulls up again, and I walked off the stones to the leaf-strewn floor of the forest. All up and down the length of the island I could hear the shouts of the men, so I lent my voice to theirs.

It must have been a startling invasion for the wild society of the island, because most of the year they live alone and in peace. Nature and bird lovers visit the island in summer, and youth groups sometimes camp for a time. But Big Blue is intended as a sanctuary so none of the birds and animals had ever heard the hullabaloo of an organized drive.

I wasn't a hundred yards into the brush when I put out a small herd of deer. I caught glimpses of their tawny hides flashing among the trunks of the trees as they leaped deadfalls and bounded away toward the open-water side of the island.

If I'd had any stomach for the killing, I might have enjoyed the maneuver, but all I could think about was how the dog must feel. I had no doubts but that Jet knew he was being hunted to the death. Perhaps at first he hadn't realized these men were after him, but now he surely knew.

I wondered how I'd feel if I was put down unarmed on an island and twelve men set ashore to round me up and kill me. It was pretty brutal, and for my own peace of mind I had to review the reasons why we were doing it. But it didn't help much, and as I neared the end of the drive I felt myself tensing against the shot which I thought would surely be forthcoming.

When I broke out onto the beach and there hadn't been any shooting, I surmised that Jet had sneaked back through the drivers again. I looked out over the water and saw the fog bank was closing in. Then, just as I was about to turn to join the men who were beginning to gather at the shore, something to my left made me turn my head.

It was Jet! He was sneaking among the boulders at the tip of the island as though contemplating flight through open water to the adjoining island.

Instinctively I dropped to a knee and raised my gun. The dog came out from among the boulders to an outcrop of rock at the water's edge. There he stood as though undecided.

Automatically the front sight of the little carbine dropped until the white bead was aimed right at the dog's heart. He hadn't seen me, didn't know I was there, never realized that death was only a trigger-squeeze away.

I held the gun on target until my arm began shaking and my vision started to blur. Jet hadn't moved. He was magnificent in silhouette.

I brought the gun down and rested my arm. I rubbed my eyes to clear my vision. Then I raised the carbine again. It was my job to kill him. In agreeing to go along on the hunt I had tacitly agreed that if the dog came within range of the gun I was carrying, I would not falter.

I had to shoot. I could not fail. If I faltered now maybe I'd falter all the rest of my life when a disagreeable task presented itself. As I kneeled there I had a fleeting glimpse, in my mind's eye, of my Dad standing in the old shed wringing the necks of his homing pigeons — killing them deliberately, one by one.

The birds had been his one luxury. He had coddled them. Perhaps they represented the freedom to fly, the freedom which Dad could never come by. He had special names for each: Fire Flash, Lightning, Rainbow, Diver. . . . Then they'd come down with a disease which was transmissable to humans. So he went to the shed and he wrung their necks, one by one even while the tears ran down his cheeks. It had been a terrible thing for him to do. But it had had to be done. And, *he'd done it!*

I settled the sights on Jet's side, took a deep breath, let half of it out, held it and started the squeeze. But in the instant before the firing pin came pinging down on the cartridge cap to set off the explosion, the little carbine moved. I can't say what made it move, or even if I intended that it should. But it moved, if only an inch, and the bullet went crashing past the dog to splinter on the boulder behind him.

Maybe chips of flying stone from the boulder stung him. Anyway, he leaped what looked to be a good twenty feet and was swimming. I was too surprised to lever another cartridge into the chamber and shoot again, but only knelt there watching while the big dog made waves as he headed out toward the open lake.

A shot from behind jarred me. I saw water spurt a few feet from Jet's head before I realized that someone behind me was shooting at him. I turned and saw that all the men were running along the beach toward me. At intervals they'd stop to shoot. Water leaped around the dog's head as though someone was pelting him with stones.

They came as far as where I was kneeling and then they also dropped to their knees to steady their aim and continued shooting. I couldn't. But no one seemed to notice. They were all too intent on trying to hit the dog.

"Shoot to the near side! Shoot to the shore side!" someone was shouting. "Get him with a ricochet!" It was Helsing, and I knew what he meant. Bullets travel at such high speed they will not enter the water but skip along the top. Shooting to the side of the dog might give a bullet a slicing angle at his head.

All the men were there by now. They knelt like an infantry squad taking deliberate aim. But Jet had gotten a good start and was a long way out. The little carbines weren't accurate over a hundred yards and most of the bullets were falling short.

"Hold your fire," Helsing called out. The guns were silent, and once again only the gulls screamed and the waves made gushing sounds as they came ashore to gurgle among the rocks. The men rose from their kneeling positions and Helsing turned to them. "Our only chance is to run him down with the boat." He turned then and started running to where the dinghys were beached.

Clambering into the little boats we rowed for the *Aldo Leopold*. Helsing was in the stern of the boat in which I was rowing. "What happened?" he asked, meaning how come I missed such an easy shot. I felt my face get red.

"I honestly don't know," I said. "I was sure I had a bead on him. I honestly don't know how I missed." It sounded weak, but it was the truth. I hadn't meant to move my arm. It was as though something I had no control over moved it for me.

By the time we were on the big boat and had the dinghys in position for towing, Jet's head was hardly more than a pinpoint of black on the lake's shining surface.

"Hurry," Helsing urged the boat captain. The big

boat came about awkwardly, but once she was straightened away from the shore she leaped to the task of running the dog down. I had taken a seat along the port side and Helsing came over and sat by me. "It's times like these," he said, "that I'd give this job to anybody who wants it even though I've only got five years to retirement."

I believed him, and I knew how he felt. Twelve men, thirteen counting me, and all armed with rifles churning along in a powerful boat to run down a practically helpless dog.

"Why don't you just let him be?" I asked.

It was a stupid question which didn't even deserve an answer, but I felt that I had to ask it. Helsing looked away out to where Jet was swimming for his life. Then he looked back at me. "What do you think would happen to the Big Blue Game Sanctuary with a killer dog running loose on it?"

I knew what would happen, and I knew that it couldn't be tolerated. "I know," I said. "I know, only . . ." I let it lie there then. What was the use? There was nothing to say. Jet just wasn't living by the rules people laid down for dogs so he had to be eliminated. Wisconsin's law was rigid, and hundreds, maybe thousands of dogs had been shot down through the years for running deer. Some wardens had shot their own dogs. So there it was. And nothing was going to change it now — not in time for Jet.

The boat was swiftly closing the gap. One of the men had climbed to the top of the cabin and was trying to steady himself for a shot by bracing his gun on the tiny handrail. He shot but I couldn't see where the bullet hit.

Helsing got up and raised his voice so he might be

heard above the roar of the engine: "Circle him. Turn him back to shore."

The man at the wheel turned toward Helsing. "I don't think we'll get to him in time. I'm afraid he's going to get into that fog bank on us."

I got to my feet to look. Jet was less than a hundred yards from the solid white wall of fog. He was swimming strong with his head high. Even his withers and his broad beaver tail were clear of the water. Labradors are excellent swimmers. Jet was the best I'd ever seen. He moved through the water like a big, black, slick seal. No wonder he had been named a champion, I thought. I would have given a lot to see him run a stake in the world champion retriever trials. I imagined there was no stake too tough. He was that big, I thought, that he could look over the top of any cover to mark a bird down and then get to it in half the time any other dog might need.

It was a race now, and the boat seemed to be losing it. The men had lined up and started shooting. The swaying boat made accuracy impossible, but with all that lead flying I felt that one of the bullets was sure to find its mark.

"Run him down," Helsing ordered the boat captain. I thought there was a look of amazement on the captain's face at Helsing's order to put the heavy bow of the boat across the dog's head. But maybe there wasn't. Bow or bullet. What difference in the end?

Everybody had crowded forward now, but I stayed in my seat. I didn't want to see it happen. Helsing didn't go forward either, but stayed on the seat beside me.

"You know how it is." He seemed to be asking my forgiveness. I knew how it was, of course, but I couldn't find it in myself to say: "Yes, I know. I know how it is."

Helsing was only doing his job, but at the moment that made no difference. I could imagine the bow of the boat crunching down on the dog's head and then I couldn't forgive him, nor myself, nor any of the men with us.

I thought how I would make a lousy soldier, or cop, or warden. When the chips were down I just didn't have the guts to kill when it was required of me.

I looked over at Helsing, but he lowered his eyes.

We were only a few feet from the fog bank and the mist was seeping in around us when a great shout went up from the men crowded together in the bow of the boat. I figured they had run the dog down, crushed him beneath the hull, that the chase, the hunt was over — the dog was dead.

It was fully a half-minute before I realized that the men had been cheering not because the dog was dead, but because he had escaped, gotten into the fog bank ahead of the boat and disappeared.

What a strange turn of events, I thought. These men, almost frantic in their efforts to kill the dog, were now cheering because he had eluded them and escaped with his life. All along, in the secret-most places of their hearts, they must have been hoping he'd get away. I'd heard of hunters like that, hunters who cheered a buck when it eluded the guns; fishermen who were happier when a big fish got away than they'd have been if they'd caught it. . . . I'd heard of it, but I'd never seen it before.

The captain put the *Aldo Leopold* straight into the fog and it was like being swathed with cotton. Visibility was cut to less than twenty feet.

"Keep circling," Helsing directed the captain.

Guiding on a compass the captain kept the boat going in ever widening circles, but it was useless.

"Cut the engine," Helsing ordered, "and everyone keep quiet. Maybe we'll hear him."

The engine sputtered and stopped. For a few seconds there was the slap of water along the boat's bow and then as her momentum decreased the sound of water subsided until there was silence. It was a ghostly experience for the thirteen of us. We held our breaths listening, but if there were any sounds to be heard the fog suffocated them. The boat lay idle for ten minutes like a craft detached from any worldly thing. The fog kept the boat alone like a ghost ship on its own tiny circle of sea.

Finally Helsing got to his feet and walked to where the captain stood still clutching the wheel. "Take her back out of the fog. We'll wait him out. He's got to come back to the island or drown."

The captain started the engine and the ghost boat became a thing alive again. He edged her around and the fog thinned and suddenly we were back under the sun. It was as shocking to see the sun as to be caught by a bright spotlight on a black night. It didn't seem possible that within the space of a hundred feet a man could ride from a world of clinging white shrouds into a world of glistening water and brilliant skies.

But that is the way it was, and Helsing ordered the boat held close enough to the island so we could survey the lake in any direction should the dog try to come back. He put two men with binoculars on the cabin, and the rest of us watched from below.

It was shortly after two o'clock and the sun was so bright we could not feel the piercing cold. I began to feel sleepy. Maybe I dozed. Helsing's voice jarred me. I thought they had spotted the dog, but he was only ordering two men to relieve those standing watch on the cabin roof.

"If he doesn't come out by dark you can bet he drowned," Helsing said. "There's no place for him to go out there. If he wants land under his paws he's got to pass us. If he doesn't, he's dead." He said it with finality. I believed him.

The fog bank didn't move. It hung out there a quarter-mile from shore as though a great, white sheet had been pulled down to screen those on the boat from the dog. The sun went low to the mainland bluffs and then hung on the tops of the cedar rims which were a black line along the horizon. Then it fell off and darkness closed swiftly around us.

"He's dead," Helsing said emphatically. "He's dead and we can go home."

So that was the end then, and the hunt was over. I pulled Muggsy close to me because I needed her. I thought about the dog swimming on and on until at last he slowly sank from sight, and I thought it might have been better if he had died from a bullet or even from having been crushed by the bow of the boat. But again, bow or bullet or oblivion in the lake. In the end, what difference did it make?

11

That should have ended it, and I thought it had. What else could happen? Helsing had said the dog was dead. My boat was in dry dock needing expensive repairs. Gear Callahan would take it in a short while anyway. Some of the villagers were laughing openly about my island search for a ghost. My brothers were ready to pounce down on me and literally haul me off to the city. Only Natalie Parish was sympathetic.

But the truth of the matter was that it hadn't ended. Not for me. Not for Chuck Morgan. Not for anybody. Maybe not even for Jet.

It wasn't a week after the boat had driven the dog into the fog bank where he presumably had drowned, when some ice fishermen had come ashore claiming they had seen Jet coming out of the mists just at dusk. Then one day a Sturgeon Bay man flew his light plane low over Big Blue Island and claimed he saw the dog standing in silhouette on the rocks just at about the place where I'd shot and missed him.

I asked Helsing about it the day he came to Killicut to give me my gear, which his men had retrieved from Gray Island. (I had boated with them to Bong Bay the night after the hunt for the dog, and then they had driven me home.)

Helsing wouldn't buy the stories which were going around. Standing on the back steps of my house, he said: "That dog is dead. Make no mistake about it. We've kept up a constant search of the islands for a sign of him. There haven't been any. He didn't make it back. He drowned."

But Helsing had hardly left Killicut when a young Coast Guardsman from Sturgeon Bay was talking in the Safe Harbor Inn and, according to Mattie Schofield, the fellow claimed he had seen the big black dog swimming in the choppy lake the day they were picking up bell buoys for winter storage.

The weeks passed and other reports kept coming in. I talked to some of the men personally and they were positive that they had seen the dog. Their stories were so convincing that I was tempted to trek out over the ice field and make another try at catching him.

The only reason I didn't go back to the islands is that some said they had seen the dog on Washington Island fifty miles north of Killicut, while others had claimed they had seen him swimming the channel at Sturgeon Bay. The two places are nearly eighty miles apart. The dog couldn't possibly have been at the two places at the same time. Somebody had to be seeing things.

Then too, many of the stories I heard began to take on a ghostly aura. One ice fisherman, for instance, said

116

the dog was fully as large as a horse and that when he had galloped across the ice he could hear the click of his paws even above the howling of the wind.

A man who had been on the ferryboat said he had seen the dog swimming and that he had been carrying a goldeneye drake in his mouth.

One ice fisherman who carried wine in his thermos instead of coffee claimed that when he saw Jet, the dog had barked at him and that the sound came across the ice like the roar of a jet airplane taking off.

Natalie Parish summed it up for me one night. I'd taken her to Safe Harbor Inn for supper because I needed her company, and she had said: "Guy, it's too good a story to give up. People don't want it to disappear. Every winter they have a different one. Sometimes it's a flying saucer. Sometimes it's a giant ghost coyote raiding the farms. Sometimes they pick a deserted house and haunt it with ghosts. It's a winter pastime, a game — telling stories like that."

What Natalie had said made sense. Looking back it did seem that every year just as winter started to clamp down on the peninsula the stories started. Maybe it was just a way for· some to take their minds off the long, cold, dreary months ahead.

Still, some of the sightings were related by men of intelligence and sound reputations. Knowing that Jet was a superior dog, a giant of his kind, physically endowed with great stamina, I found myself half-believing that he might still be alive. I tried explaining to Natalie why I thought it possible that the dog had survived. It only made her angry.

"For heaven's sake, be realistic, Guy!" she said. "You figure you can solve all your problems just by catching that dog. That's why you don't want to admit the dog

117

is dead. You're afraid to admit it. As soon as you admit he's dead you've got nothing left, you've got no place to go except to find a job and forget about owning a fleet."

I had to admit to myself that what she said was logical, but I didn't admit it to her. But I dropped it, because I had troubles enough and I didn't want to lose her. She was about the only real friend I had left.

The day after Natalie and I had had supper together, my brother John descended on me. I won't go into it, but all day he argued about taking me back to Milwaukee and shutting up the house or renting it out.

"You'll starve up here," John kept saying.

That was ridiculous, of course. I might not make much money, but above all I wouldn't starve.

"You'll kill yourself with your harebrained schemes," he kept repeating.

The only answer I had to that was the old cliché: "Nothing ventured, nothing gained."

"You'll turn into a bum like Bill Bratton or Luke Morrisson," was another one of his arguments.

I didn't let that pass. "Bratton and Morrisson aren't bums," I insisted. "If they are, then all the old fishermen around here are bums. They're just old men who want to be left alone to live out the rest of their lives as best they can. They're two wonderful people. They've never hurt a person in their whole lives."

He didn't mention Bratton or Morrisson again, but concentrated on trying to show me how my life would become a wasted effort if I didn't put it to some better purpose than dreaming.

Mostly I let him talk, and at last it was like hearing a broken record. When he saw I wouldn't argue he finally quieted and then I asked: "What are you going to do? Get the law in here and force me to go to Milwau-

118

kee with you? Kick me out of the house? Tie me up and throw me into the trunk of your car and truck me south like a calf or a pig?"

I think that sort of got him thinking. He seemed to take a second look at me and maybe he realized I wasn't a kid any longer and that he just couldn't shove me around and treat me as though I were a possession instead of an individual in my own right.

Legally, of course, I didn't have a leg to stand on. I was in John's custody and if he wanted to get tough he could make me do his bidding or make me wish that I had. But I didn't think he'd go that far.

Actually he was a fine brother and I loved him. He was only trying to look out for my welfare, and I realized it. But I had to get it through to him that I was almost nineteen and that ever since our parents had died I'd been thinking for myself and I wasn't ready now to let someone else do it for me.

He had to get back the next day and we parted friends when I promised positively that if things didn't change for the better by spring I'd give up the idea of making my way alone on the peninsula and come to Milwaukee. I suppose he thought he had me there, because what could I do except maybe work for Messmer in the woods in the winter or get a job at Sturgeon in the shipyards. What could I do?

Next day Messmer put me on. Maybe he felt sorry for me, but maybe not. He said that good help was hard to find, and since I could handle a power saw with the best of the old-timers, could I come to work the next day?

It wasn't a solution because I would never make enough during the logging season to accumulate anywhere near the kind of money I needed to keep the boat. But I had to eat, and I had to buy fuel, and I was honor-bound to pay some rent though part of the house belonged to me. It was a good feeling to have a couple of bucks in my pocket so I could take Natalie out once in a while.

Then too, I liked working in the woods. The deer always came around to browse on the tops of the trees we felled. The men were always jovial and playing jokes. Each day I could feel my muscles getting tighter and stronger under my shirt. Food tasted better and sleep was a wonderful, welcome thing after swinging a twenty-pound saw all day.

I got up before dawn the next morning so as to be in front of the post office where Messmer picked up his crew by sunup. I had planned on taking Muggsy with me because she was no trouble in the woods and so I wouldn't have to keep her locked up all day. But when I was ready to go and I called to her she didn't get up from the rug and only lay looking at me.

"Come on, Muggsy. Come on," I urged. She only whined and put her head back down to the blanket.

At once I had a sick feeling. I hurried over, but her nose was moist, her eyes clear, her coat shiny, and her ears were cool to the touch so I knew she didn't have a fever.

"What is it, Muggsy?" I asked. She rolled over slowly and then it hit me, and I wondered how I could have been so blind as not to have noticed it before. I put my hand on her stomach and held it there.

Jeeze, I thought, she's that far along that it could happen any day.

"Muggsy, Muggsy, why didn't you tell me?" Then I realized how ridiculous I sounded.

120

Well, it was no wonder Natalie Parish said I was so misty-eyed over my dream I couldn't see anything else in the world. Here my own dog was on the very verge of having pups and I'd never suspected that it was going to happen.

But how? When? I hadn't noticed anything. Then something John had said to me hit me right between the eyes with the full impact truth can sometimes have. He had said: "You're getting to be a menace to yourself because you're so wrapped up in this crazy scheme of yours that you don't even know what's going on in your own kitchen. The place looks like a pigpen! You're like a man possessed! I'll bet you even sleep with your clothes on!"

Well, it wasn't that bad, but I could realize now how far out of touch I'd been because all I had had on my mind was the boat and the dream of some day forming the Killicut Crew Company.

I kept my hand on Muggsy's stomach until I felt life, felt the puppies moving around inside her. Then I got up and went to the basement to get a box for her to use in birthing. I set the box on its side so she could crawl into it and lined it with old rags. Then I put down water and filled her food dish and had to run all the way to the post office to catch the Messmer truck.

The pups were born that night. I didn't get any sleep. I sat in front of the box watching, and the first pup came at exactly nine-thirty. It gave her trouble, and I wanted to reach down and help with it, but she nosed my hand away and with a final grunt of half-pain and half-relief, she brought the pup into the world. Then through the night, at irregular intervals, she gave birth to another and another until there were nine.

I couldn't bring myself to go back to the woods the

next day, so for the first time in my life I played sick. Then when I was sure Muggsy was all right and the puppies were all dry, warm, and healthy, I did something I should have done weeks ago. I called Chuck Morgan.

He got there right after supper and said he had flown to Green Bay and rented a car and driven up from there. We sat at the kitchen table and under the light his white hair and his white mustache shone like new snow under a bright moon.

All of a sudden then it seemed incongruous that a multimillionaire brewer should be sitting across a kitchen table from me. It also seemed fantastic that a man with so many big business interests should find so much time to devote to the search for a single dog. But some men are like that, I suppose.

Anyway I told him the whole story about Jet, and I told him about all the stories which were making the rounds, and I ended it by telling how Helsing was certain the dog was dead.

When I finished he just sat there, and the only sound was a little hiss of steam from the tea kettle which I'd left on a low burner so we could have fresh coffee. Finally he put a hand to his face and rubbed it around as though trying to erase the wrinkles in his forehead, to scrub away the crow's feet at the corners of his eyes.

Finally he put his hand down and said: "Guy, if John Helsing said that Jet is dead, then I believe that he is dead. I've known Helsing's reputation for years. He wouldn't say a thing like that unless he was absolutely sure of what he was saying."

Hearing Morgan say it made it terribly final. I hadn't been able to make myself believe, not with the same conviction with which Morgan was now accepting

Jet's death. It seemed now, however, I could believe it because someone had said it who knew both the dog and Helsing, someone who had a stake in the dog's life.

We just sat there then, letting the truth sink in so it would become a part of what we knew and not something upsetting our minds with its newness and strangeness. Then I remembered the pups. Getting up I walked to where the wooden box was almost hidden back of the kitchen sink. I hadn't told Morgan about the pups and he gave me a surprised look when I motioned and said: "Come here."

He came over and looked down and I picked up a flashlight off the drainboard of the sink and turned it on the nursing pups. For a while he just stood there. Then he bent over and picked up a pup and put his forefinger to the little one's chin where the white blaze was plain to see. The blind puppy, feeling the finger, searched for it with his wet little mouth.

Morgan put the pup back down and picked up another. Again he touched the tiny patch of white on the animal's chin. One by one he picked up all nine of the youngsters and each time he touched the white spot before putting the pup down. Then he turned to me and all he said was one word: "Jet!"

Standing there in the kitchen I could hear again how Muggsy howled and I could see her running from her seat on the *Killicut* and leaping from the stern into the night.

"Yes, it was Jet," I said.

"Then he really isn't dead," Morgan said.

At first I didn't get it because I didn't know how he meant it. He saw my surprise so, pointing to the pups, he said: "Jet is there. In the pups. In the end it is the only way."

EPILOGUE

That was all a couple of years ago that we stood in the kitchen, looking down at Muggsy's pups. I'm still on the peninsula. In the spring I lease out my boat to the federal government to help clean up the alewives which pollute the beaches, in the summer I take out sport fishermen for trout and salmon and bass, and in the fall I do some commercial fishing.

I've got the *Killicut* free and clear and I've got a down payment made on a second boat because the lake is teeming with fish. I'm sure it won't be many more seasons before the lake will be opened to commercial fishing.

Usually when I'm out on the water there are two black dogs with me. One is Muggsy, of course, and the other has a white blaze on his chin and is twice as big as his mother. He's a magnificent dog.

The other pups?

Morgan wouldn't have it any other way but that I take three hundred dollars apiece for them. He claimed they were worth twice that to him.

And Jet?

People are still seeing him. Hunters come in each fall talking about a big, black dog which went galloping away over the islands. Fishermen say they see him swimming out of a fog bank. Sometimes people a hundred miles distant from each other claim to have seen him on the same night.

Maybe. Maybe not.

I thought I saw him once, but then it might have been the reflection of a big boulder cast against a fog bank.

Customers aboard the boat often ask me what I know about the story, because it has been in all the papers. I don't spoil it for them by saying I'm sure the dog is dead. Instead I tell them the story about how Jet's pups were born and I laughingly say they were the gift of a ghost. And, they like that.

Natalie? She's wearing my ring and I can feel it on her finger when she takes my hand in hers and tells me how marvelous everything is.